Death By Grand Jury

AND OTHER D.C. STORIES

Death By Grand Jury

AND OTHER D.C. STORIES

Bruce Clarke

Columbus, Ohio

This book is a work of fiction. The names, characters and events in this book are the products of the author's imagination or are used fictitiously. Any similarity to real persons living or dead is coincidental and not intended by the author.

Death By Grand Jury and Other D.C. Stories

Published by Gatekeeper Press
2167 Stringtown Rd, Suite 109
Columbus, OH 43123-2989
www.GatekeeperPress.com

Copyright © 2018 by Bruce Clarke
All rights reserved. Neither this book, nor any parts within it may be sold or reproduced in any form or by any electronic or mechanical means, including information storage and retrieval systems without permission in writing from the author. The only exception is by a reviewer, who may quote short excerpts in a review.

ISBN (paperback): 9781642373790
eISBN: 9781642372052

Printed in the United States of America

Contents

Sweet Dreams Called Leavin' 1
Birds Of A Feather 25
Fresh Eyes 49
Death By Grand Jury 69
A Walk Down North Capitol Street 105
Loveboat 123
The Four F's 145
A Shooting on R Street 157
A Day in The Life 171

For my family

Sweet Dreams Called Leavin'

Tommy Agee ground the tip of his last Marlboro into one of the ashtrays flanking the entrance to the Superior Court building and gave the guards a thumbs-up as he went inside. He wasn't sure why he made the gesture; in fact, his stomach was knotted and he was tired of playing the waiting game. He made his way through the security station in the lobby and was collecting his wallet and keys when he noticed Judge Fazio's courtroom clerk moving toward him, bristling with purpose. Miss Jackson's face wore the stern, disapproving look he'd become so familiar with during his maiden voyage as a trial lawyer. Agee shoved his possessions into his pockets and turned toward her, knowing the jury had reached a verdict.

"Hello, Miss Jackson," he began, but she interrupted him.

"Mr. Agee, sir, we have a note from the jury. I called and left you three messages. *Please*, sir, report to the courtroom right away."

She was using what he called her Long-Suffering Clerk's Voice. It was reserved for counsel like him: counsel who failed to grasp the importance of the protocols she and Judge Fazio had devised to ensure the steady forward movement of cases on the judge's docket. It was a strong, clear voice tinged with disdain.

Agee observed for the record—his completely internal record of events that had transpired thus far in the case of

United States v. Willie R. Mayo—that Miss Jackson had again managed to use the word "sir" in a way that reversed its usual connotation. It was one of many frustrating aspects of the case that had led to Agee's first jury trial. In fact it seemed to him that since the day he volunteered to represent Mayo *pro bono*, Miss Jackson had made scolding him, about matters both large and small, the main thrust of her business. This wasn't what life had led him to expect, and he didn't take it well. Her condescending manner made him angry, and the need to contain that anger, to mute his response to her hostility time and again for the sake of the measured politeness expected in his new profession, made him tense and led him to inhale more Marlboros than he'd like.

Not that the experience would otherwise have been tension-free, Agee thought as he followed Miss Jackson toward Fazio's courtroom. In addition to the not-inconsiderable stress generated by any first jury trial, this one came with an extra, high-octane stressor: an innocent client. Of course, Agee had reminded himself time and again that it was not the lawyer's function to play God and judge whether a client was innocent or guilty. But clinging to that time-honored law school dictum offered him no solace. Deep down in his fevered gut, Agee had long ago concluded his client had not committed the felonies he was charged with. Or, as Mayo himself put it, "They crazy—I ain't arm-robbed nobody."

Given the stakes, Agee had prepared for the trial like nothing before. But he'd also looked forward to the contest. He'd resolved to become a trial lawyer, and was excited by the prospect of emerging triumphant from a professional experience certain to be more challenging than anything he'd encountered at law school or the firm. Plus, it was a tribute of sorts—perhaps to his law firm credentials—that the court had appointed him to such a serious case. At this point, as he followed Miss Jackson down the buffed and shined Superior Court hallways, he still hoped to prevail. But he felt more like a boxer in the fifteenth round than a lawyer changing his career path.

All in all, the trial had been a harrowing experience. For openers, the prosecutor, Assistant United States Attorney "Bullet Bob" McCallum, and the trial judge, former prosecutor Vincent Fazio, had much in common. Fazio was a veteran judge with a hotwire temper that led him to snap pencils when disturbed, and Agee had disturbed him on day one. The judge had a reputation for fairness, but no tolerance for the fumblings of novice counsel. The extent to which Agee's fumblings had upset Fazio during the trial was likely reflected in his dream the night before closing arguments. In it he had fallen repeatedly to a courtroom floor littered with broken lead pencils while arguing Mayo's case to the jury. Every time he'd tried to make an important point, he tripped over a yellow Number Two pencil shard and lost his bearings.

Bullet Bob was no picnic either. Unlike Fazio, Bob was *supposed* to be Agee's adversary, so there was a systemic justification of sorts for the keen blend of sarcasm and hostility he directed at Agee. Also unlike Fazio, who figured to remain on the bench for life, Bob was finishing the standard prosecutor tour of duty and was on his way to bigger things. He would soon become Assistant General Counsel to the Maryland legislature's Judiciary Committee, a fact he managed to tell Agee ten minutes into their first meeting, shortly after Agee mentioned Mayo's case might go to trial.

"Listen, do what you like," Bob had responded while

adjusting the case files on his desk, "But I'll tell you, at this point in my Superior Court career I could sleepwalk through the trial naked and still convict your client. This is a two-eyewitness case, you know."

Agee knew, but didn't blink. He'd already investigated the case, and learned there were problems with the eyewitness testimony. One witness had been drinking before the crime went down, and the other was more nervous than a bird near cats.

"But frankly," Bob continued, "I'm up to my neck in homicides these days and so I'd like to avoid going to trial in a dog robbery case; it's almost not worth my time. And I see your guy has no prior record, so I'd be willing to offer him the opportunity to plead to only one life count." Robbery While Armed would do nicely, Bob felt, and Fazio could be expected to lop a few years off Mayo's sentence in return for the plea. "Bottom line," Bob advised Agee, "you'd be doing your client a huge favor and, in my eyes, acting most professionally by persuading the two-bit hoodlum to cop to the count."

This offer was given context by a thought unspoken but shared by both of them, which was that if Mayo chose trial by jury and went down on all counts, Fazio would measure the kid's sentence in decades.

While riding the elevator with the silent Miss Jackson, Agee reviewed his performance at trial. He was not yet a full-blown criminal trial lawyer, he knew that now. He'd taken the standard prep courses in law school, getting his feet wet handling petty misdemeanors—disorderly conduct, sexual solicitation, minor league theft—under the supervision of academics. It was exciting, the stakes were low, and it was easy to end run the overworked D.A.s in most cases. But felonies were from a universe undreamed of in academe, and he'd made some mistakes along the way. All in all, he thought, he probably shouldn't have volunteered for such a serious case.

Still, the way to become a great trial lawyer—for he'd decided to walk in the shoes of the Clarence Darrows, Melvin Bellis, and F. Lee Baileys of the world—was to try cases. Certainly becoming a trial lawyer seemed a lot more exciting than work at the firm, which to its credit had granted him a leave of absence to finish up his courtroom adventure. But the firm also wanted him back and in his proper seat the minute he was done. It was a plush seat, in a venerable firm. The problem was, life at D.C.'s Levy, Conklin & Dunne office was boring. There were the usual compensations; nevertheless, it was boredom he'd tried to escape with a wild ride through the bedlam that was Superior Court. It wasn't like he'd been motivated by excess empathy for the poor, the lost, the drugged, the violent, and the deviant—the Catch of the Day, as the marshals called them. No, it was a combination of ennui and ambition that led him to the cellblock holding Willie Mayo.

And yet it was more than that. Inhaling deeply as they left the elevator, he felt something else in his chest besides the strangely comforting post-Marlboro burning sensation. It was a kind of realization; the painful kind that started mental but played itself out in the body: he'd never really been tested before. So far he'd gotten by without engaging his entire being in an all-or-nothing struggle for something held dear and beyond price. So far, but as the sensation in Agee's chest moved to his heart, he knew he'd avoided such struggles by living life around the edges. Dust on the fringe of life; the phrase leapt into his head. Philosophy major in college, three unexciting years of law school, a year spent reviewing contracts at the firm. In short this trial was the first real test of his mettle, of what he could give and what he could take, of what he was capable of in the clinches. It had been a tough test, but everything considered, he still felt confident he'd prevail.

He followed Miss Jackson through the windowless door to the courtroom and watched her move briskly toward the clerk's desk. Seconds later she was on the phone, letting all aggrieved parties know that defense counsel had at last been located. It would take a few minutes for Fazio and McCallum to arrive in the room, and longer for the marshals to retrieve Mayo from the netherworld of the cellblock, so Agee still had significant time on his hands.

Within seconds he began filling that time by worrying about the verdict, something he'd been doing for almost five hours now. It was perhaps the worst part of the entire experience: the time when confidence ebbed, doubts surfaced, and he began to fear things hadn't gone so well after all. A dark cloud of despair would then pass through his mind and dash his hopes for an acquittal.

Each time those unpleasant thoughts surfaced, the face of Juror 1642 appeared in his mind's eye. Once 1642 appeared, he couldn't get her image out of his head until he'd rerun the moment when he'd decided not to strike her from the jury. And once he'd rerun that film, his imagination insisted on playing the sequel. This was the film of the verdict, in which 1642 stood in the jury box, unfolded a small yellow piece of paper, locked eyes with Agee and spoke the word "guilty."

He'd taken a number of flat-out chances during the trial, but allowing 1642 to remain on the jury was the biggest. It happened at that point in the voir dire when potential jurors are asked a series of questions designed to plumb the depths of their impartiality. A key question in the litany, one that led about fifteen people to line up at the bench for individual questioning by Fazio and the lawyers, was "Have any of you ever been the victim of a crime, a witness to a crime, or charged with a crime?"

1642 had answered "yes" to the question by raising her hand, and at the bench told Fazio, Agee and Bullet Bob that she'd been a crime victim three times. Three times! Fazio asked her to elaborate on how she'd been had, and she'd replied in a quiet, neutral tone, "I was robbed, my car was stolen, and once someone tried to break into my house."

Agee took a close look at her while she spoke. She was wearing small gold earrings and a matching necklace over a medium blue blouse. Her hair was short and neat. She looked to be in her forties but it was hard to tell how deep into the decade she was. Her face had the tight, smooth skin of youth but was given a trace of age and severity by prominent wrinkles near the mouth.

Unseasoned as he was, Agee knew why defense lawyers had qualms about seating crime victims on a jury. Victims spent time in police stations, bonding with investigating officers and soaking up their singular perspective on how the justice system worked. As such, defenders viewed them as prone to presume defendants guilty, believe all police witnesses, and argue for conviction in the jury room.

Still, Agee had reasoned, this was only the conventional wisdom of the defense bar—formed over time, based on experience, but surely subject to exception. The thing to do was find out whether it applied to the real-life person who'd answered yes to the crime victim question and wound up standing nervously before the bench, fingering the buttons on her blouse. This was done by asking follow-up questions designed to reveal attitudes rather than facts. One such question was, "Were you satisfied with how the police handled those cases?" and Bullet Bob posed it right away.

"Yes, I was satisfied," 1642 answered, and Bob relaxed. Agee followed up with "Did any of those cases go to court?"

"Only one, it was the robbery," she said.

"What was the outcome?" asked Bob.

"The man pled guilty, so I didn't really get that involved," replied 1642. That was good, thought Agee. Less involvement meant less contact, less taint. But still, a three-time crime victim was almost universally considered to be inclined toward the prosecution. He could sense Fazio and McCallum waiting for him to try to strike 1642 from the panel for lack of impartiality.

Anticipating the strike, Fazio moved to cut things short by asking her the payoff question. "Now, despite that experience, do you think you would be capable of giving the defendant in this case a fair trial, and rendering a verdict based solely on the evidence?" Some judges phrased this query as a leading question, in order to suggest to the juror they'd prefer a "yes" answer, one that would move things along. But to his credit, Fazio asked the question straight.

"Yes I can," replied 1642 without pause.

This response was sufficient in law for Fazio to reject any challenge to 1642's impartiality, making it certain she'd sit on the jury unless Agee used one of his peremptory challenges to remove her. As they all knew, a peremptory could be used to knock a prospective juror off the jury for almost any reason, including a lawyer's gut-level hunch that the juror wouldn't be receptive to his case. Fazio and Bob both eyeballed Agee immediately after 1642's response, as if they fully expected him to use a peremptory to get rid of her. Bullet Bob even blurted out, "Your move, Mr. Agee," before he could stop himself.

So the judge and Bullet Bob made brief eye contact when Agee replied, "I do not wish to strike the juror." He knew that in their eyes he'd just proven himself a rank amateur—but he also felt they were wrong. Mired in convention, they'd missed something he felt was earnest and true in the way she uttered the words "Yes I can." There was a firmness, a resolute timbre in the way she said those words, that sent him a signal that despite her experience she would bend over backwards to be fair to young Mayo. More than that, Agee had gotten the sense, through a slight edge he detected in her voice, that she was determined to show one and all in that busy building just how fair and impartial she could be. Maybe, he surmised, she'd been struck from other juries during her time of service in Superior Court. Maybe she hadn't yet been given a chance to perform the very duty she'd been summoned for. Maybe she was anxious to overcome the system's doubts in her integrity. A host of maybes, but the timbre of her voice sent them all coursing through Agee's mind at once and he decided not to strike her. At the time, it seemed to him that 1642 had responded by pulling her shoulders back a bit and exhaling, and he'd taken that as a good sign.

Now, Agee wondered about his choice. He'd begun second-guessing himself as soon as he told Dennis Moore, an experienced public defender, about the move during a break in the trial.

"Three times, ooh man that's one hell of a gamble," Moore had responded before sensing Agee's discomfort and adding, "Bold move, though. You never know." But it was too late.

Moore's skill with juries was well known, and his response had been a blow.

Standing now in the back of the courtroom, a safe distance from Miss Jackson, Agee's insides tightened as he recalled these events. He distracted himself as best he could by focusing on the austere, functional décor of the arena in which he stood. Like all such arenas, this one had been designed to ensure jurors weren't diverted from their task, which was to sift through the evidence with care and reach a just verdict. The law defined a just verdict as one based on reason, not emotion, for it assumed that only a rational process could lead to a just result.

It became clear to Agee how every aspect of the courtroom's design had been crafted in support of this goal of pure reasonableness in juror deliberations. The dark oak paneling was intended to lend weight and substance to the proceedings. The plain wooden jury box incorporated not one feature that might cause a juror's mind to wander. The raised throne-like bench allowed a serious black-robed judge to watch the entire room at all times. The national and state flags even had replicas of eagles perched at the tips of their staffs, as if they too were there to scrutinize the evidence. Finally, the smooth marble wall behind the judge's bench bore no inscription whatsoever, the designers having decided unadorned marble would send jurors a more dignified message than any words humans might inscribe on it. In sum, every feature of the room was selected to promote the goals of order, seriousness, and deliberative thought, and thus to guard against the infusion of strong feelings—emotions—into the jurors' deliberations.

It was of course the trial lawyers' job to upend all this, to sabotage and destroy the intent of the designers, by injecting as much raw passion into the proceedings as they could get away with. Agee and McCallum both knew this, and despite his worries Agee smiled slightly as he recalled moments in the trial when, despite Fazio's best efforts, they'd done just that.

Bob had scored first, managing to engineer a teary-eyed breakdown of Ingrid, one of the two victims, as she described how the lone gunman had burst into her friend Oscar's apartment and stuck a gun in her face before proceeding to rob them. That really got the jury's back up. Its sympathy for the witness, and its anger at the sudden savage assault, were palpable in the room. But then Agee's strategy on cross of letting her go on and on—and on still longer—about how scared she was during the offense began to work, and the feeling in the courtroom slowly turned from anger to curiosity about the witness's state of mind, and then to worry—worry that the intrusion and assault had so petrified the woman that her subsequent identification of Mayo as the robber was suspect.

Then, later in the trial, after the testimony of Oscar and the detectives had restored credibility to his case, Bullet Bob's cross of Mayo's sister Shawnell had offended the jurors. At first they directed a cold, judgmental anger at the defendant's sister, seemingly revealed by Bob to be lying under oath. The Bullet's rat-a-tat-tat questioning had gotten Shawnell so confused on cross she mixed her dates up, allowing him to use a handy prop—the calendar on Fazio's bench—to confront her with the unquestionable Julian fact that, while she'd just given her brother a perfect alibi for Tuesday, June 19th, the crime had gone down on Wednesday, the 20th.

Figuring the jury assumed Shawnell had become confused about the dates because she was lying to cover for a guilty brother, Agee had decided to strike back quickly. Luckily, Bob had gone out of his way to elicit from Shawnell that their other brother, Derrick, had been with her and Willie at the time in question, but had not been called to testify. Here McCallum was thinking ahead to closing argument, when he'd score points by asking the jury to conclude the only reason Derrick wasn't called was that his testimony wouldn't have supported the defense. This gave Agee the opportunity to deflect the jury's anger from Shawnell to Bullet Bob himself, with a single question and answer:

Q. Now, Shawnell, do you know why your brother Derrick hasn't been called as a witness at this trial?

A. Yeah, he in a mental hospal. He don't think too good, so they got him hospalized.

Which was the explanation Agee knew was coming, and made the jury see Bob's devastating cross-examination of Shawnell in an altogether different light, the harsh light of public humiliation of a young girl who didn't think too good either. So the anger boomeranged back on Bob, and another strong feeling, borne of sympathy for an underdog witness, spread through the room. That was a sweet moment for the defense. It kept the case up for grabs even as Mayo's alibi defense fell apart.

Which most alibi defenses did, according to Dennis Moore. As the PD put it, "absent theatre tickets, there's an inherent difficulty in proving, months later, that you were someplace else at the time the crime went down. And I've never yet had a client who could find those theatre tickets." Worse yet, counseled Moore, most alibi witnesses were like Shawnell, relatives bent on sheltering a loved one on trial, and thus easily depicted as stretching things, if not outright lying—which they often were.

Suddenly, a voice rang out in the room and yanked Agee's mind back to the present. It was Miss Jackson. "I sort of liked your closing argument," she said. This offer of casual conversation was a first on her part, and Agee wasn't sure how to react.

"Oh, thanks. We'll see," he replied, moving closer to her desk, which jutted out to one side of the judge's bench.

"Believe me, I've seen hundreds of them. McCallum was fired up, but he always talks down a bit to the jury," she added while inspecting one of the thicker case files before her.

"Good, I hope they were offended," said Agee.

"Most prosecutors do that," she observed, getting downright chatty. "I think it's because they really don't trust juries. You know, they worry they're gonna fall sucker for that reasonable doubt thing . . . . Anyway, I'd best finish this stack up or I'll be here all night."

Miss Jackson removed her glasses and rubbed her eyes, and for the first time Agee felt some form of personal connection with her. She didn't hate him, or the other lawyers she scolded, he thought. No, she was a dedicated public servant working her way through endless stacks of dull brown files in order to keep the system running. Obviously, the lawyers' plodding slowness was driving her mad, breaking her stride and causing her to work even longer hours.

"This is my first felony trial," he blurted, thankful she'd assumed human form.

"No kidding, Sherlock," she said, reverting to a tone of voice Agee was more familiar with. Snap went the connection. Anger flashed through him and he moved away from her.

He returned to counsel table and fussed with his own files while he calmed down. Soon he recalled Miss Jackson's compliment, which led him to re-live the closings. Before the arguments, Fazio had warned him, "You can't express your own personal belief in the innocence of the defendant, because then the trial turns into a credibility contest between you and Mr. McCallum. So don't say, 'I believe he's innocent,' or Bob'll be all over you." Agee had thanked him for the advice and made a mental note not to say the words "I believe." But like the stars of the trial bar he'd been reading about, he planned to communicate to the jury—without saying the taboo words, but using every other device available to him—his total, unshakable belief in the righteousness of Mayo's cause.

Bullet Bob had played his role to the hilt during final argument, becoming a living embodiment of the community's rage as he retold the story of the crime and urged the jurors to punish the offense committed by the slump-shouldered defendant sitting before them. What better evidence could they want, asked Bob, than the testimony of eyewitnesses, *two* eyewitnesses, who pointed to Mayo without pause when asked if they saw the robber in the courtroom?

"And as for the defendant's alibi evidence, it was so pathetic and contrived," Bob told the jurors, "that it may as well count as part of the *government's* case. Forget reasonable doubt, the state has proven its case beyond a shadow of a doubt." The Bullet had spoken with supreme confidence, and despite Miss Jackson's comments, Agee remembered well that by the time the D.A. sat down, everyone sensed the jury was ready to convict.

That thought was enough to scoot Agee's mind back to the present, where he occupied himself working up a head of steam at the marshals for taking so long to get Mayo from the central cellblock. He started to complain to Miss Jackson about the delay, then thought better of it. Instead he sat, closed his eyes and rubbed his temples. Soon his thoughts drifted back to the trial.

He'd prepared all weekend in order to be able to deliver a fully orchestrated closing like the Bullet had. In it, he'd asked the jurors a series of questions, hoping to awaken in them the fear of convicting an innocent man. His mantra was that the vaunted eyewitnesses were also the terrified victims in the case, victims who'd been dazed and distracted as the robbery went down, and so unable to focus clearly on the intruder. Hadn't Oscar had a beer or two just before the robbery, and been drowsy when the event occurred? Hadn't they seen how upset Ingrid had become as she re-lived the offense? Couldn't they imagine, then, her state of mind when it actually happened? Did a state of mind like that make for an identification they could rely on? Sure, the twosome had fingered Mayo every time out, but if they'd been wrong the first time, hadn't they just been repeating their initial mistake?

"In fact," he'd asked them, "didn't the government's own evidence raise a series of doubts in your mind, doubts that nag at your soul and leave you lacking the moral certainty needed to convict?"

He had ended by demanding they "return a fair verdict, a just verdict, a verdict of *not guilty* on behalf of William Mayo." It had been a summation straight from the heart, marred too often by his nervousness, but by its end he felt he'd thwarted the Bullet's effort. He'd clung to that hope hour after hour as he waited for the verdict, wandering the courthouse square and turning himself into a Marlboro Man.

Finally, just as he began thinking he'd been dropped through a chute to hell, doomed to spend all eternity waiting for the verdict, Agee heard the metal clang of the cellblock door. The clang meant the marshals had at last brought Mayo from the basement cellblock, where he'd waited all day, to the tiny holding cell behind the courtroom. Agee walked across the well of the court to the door leading to the cell, shouldered it open, and edged inside. The cell itself took up half the room. The remainder barely held him and one well-nourished marshal.

Mayo stood leaning against the bars, his thin six-foot frame slightly stooped as always. With his light brown complexion, short-cut Afro, blue eyes and County Mayo moniker, it seemed to Agee the whole sad history of black and white relations had played itself out in his client's name and body.

Mayo usually looked down or off to the side when Agee spoke to him, and didn't say much, so Agee always took a low-key, casual approach with him. "How's it going," he said, and Mayo replied with his standard-issue "Guess I'll make it," spoken in a flat tone to the hard floor.

"What's taking them so long?" he added quickly. "The marshal said they got a verdick."

"That's right; they have a verdict. They'll bring you into the courtroom after the judge gets here. After they bring the jury in—"

"What about the dude with the suspenders?"

"He'll be there too." Mayo was referring to Bullet Bob, who tended to snap his suspenders after he damaged a witness on cross-examination.

"Can I still plead insanity or something?" said Mayo.

"No, I'm afraid not," said Agee.

"Just kidding. I still got a sweet dream called leavin' this place."

For a second Agee pictured Mayo walking the concrete

mile back to his home, an outsized grin on his happy face. In fact he'd only been locked up three days. Fazio had left him out on bail until the second day of trial, but on that day he and his sister had arrived at the courtroom fifteen minutes late, and the judge wasted no time locking him up.

Agee started to ask Mayo if his mother planned to be in court for the verdict, but then checked himself, thinking it unlikely. She'd watched part of the first day, but that had either been enough or all she could take, because she hadn't been seen since. Instead, Agee decided to reassure his client that everything would turn out all right, but before he could do so Miss Jackson stuck her head in the door and hissed "the judge is on the bench." That left Agee with just enough time to say "See you out there—it'll be all right" and ease out of the tiny space so the marshal had room to unlock the cell door.

"Bring in the jury please, Bailiff," barked Fazio as soon as Agee entered the courtroom. Bullet Bob was already there, and seconds later the marshal led Mayo over to the defendant's chair, where he sat next to Agee. Then they all waited, silent and anxious, like troops awaiting an assault. A moment later, a door in the wall opposite the defense table swung open. The bailiff appeared; Miss Jackson said "All rise," and suddenly they were knee-deep in ritual. Everyone stood, hands at sides and eyes toward the door, facing the jury as it entered the room. The jurors walked in slowly, single file, their faces focused and serious.

All in all they were a nondescript lot. More old than young, more women than men, all conventionally dressed and groomed. None of them were likely to attract attention in a crowd. The brightly clothed, the wildly styled, the too neat, the not neat enough, and the wearers of pins or buttons reflecting too strong a connection with a cause, any cause, were not to be found among them. For completely different reasons, Agee, McCallum, and Fazio had wound up striking them all from the jury. The folklore said the strikes left most juries a collection of conformists, but as Agee watched these twelve people move carefully to their seats, he observed details in each one's walk, dress and demeanor that made him think otherwise.

The first juror to enter was the heavy-set, dark-haired secretary with a slight limp. She was wearing a brown dress and bifocals. She glanced at the well of the courtroom, in the general direction of counsel table, but didn't make eye contact with anyone. Before Agee could worry about her he saw Juror 1642 a few jurors back, and something in him surged and blurred the room.

When the surge had passed though him and he was able to refocus, Agree saw her adjust her purse as she crossed from the door to the jury box, then look over toward Mayo for a second as she took her seat. He wondered if a folded yellow paper, like the one he'd dreamed about, was in the purse.

After the jurors were seated, Fazio announced he had received a note from them revealing they had reached a verdict.

"Is that the case, ladies and gentlemen of the jury? Have you reached a unanimous verdict in this case, on all counts in the indictment?"

They all nodded.

"Very well," the judge continued, "would the foreman, ah—foreperson—of the jury please rise?" There was a slight pause, enough time to draw breath in and let it out again, then Juror 1642 stood in the box. Surprisingly, Agee felt nothing in particular as she rose. It was as if he were watching the unfolding of a scene he knew by heart.

"Would the clerk please deliver a copy of the verdict to the court?" Fazio intoned, and within seconds Miss Jackson was making a dignified cross to the jury box. 1642 placed the verdict form in Jackson's outstretched hand. It consisted of two pages of questions about the nine offenses, questions that could be answered "guilty" or "not guilty" with a simple check mark.

As Miss Jackson strode back to Fazio's bench holding the form, Agee managed a glance at McCallum, who was sitting forward, hands folded, straight-backed as always. Mayo, in contrast, was all angles and shoulder blades. He sat to Agee's right, hunched over the oak defense table, tracing the grain of the wood with his index finger.

Fazio took the form from Miss Jackson and placed it before him on the bench. He looked quickly through both pages, nodded, and said "Very well" to Miss Jackson in a voice that gave nothing away. "Very well" was Jackson's signal to return the papers to 1642 for the formal announcement of the verdict.

As she did this, the phrase "Surely goodness and mercy shall follow me all the days of my life" zinged through Agee's head and repeated itself like a nonsense rhyme until Fazio said "Mr. Mayo, please rise and face the jury, sir."

This was it. Mayo stood and looked at 1642, who stood clutching the forms. Agee and Bullet Bob got up at the same time. Then Fazio continued, "With respect to Count One of the indictment, Robbery While Armed, how do you find the defendant, members of the jury: Guilty or Not Guilty?"

"Guilty," 1642 said, and a short, sharp breath escaped from Mayo's lips.

"With respect to Count Two," continued Fazio, "Burglary While Armed, how do you find the defendant, members of the jury: Guilty or Not Guilty?"

"Guilty," 1642 replied. Suddenly Mayo's knees buckled and he fell to the floor, moaning the word "no" on his way down.

Fazio responded at once to this departure from courtroom decorum. "Please remain standing, Mr. Mayo, until the jury has rendered its verdict," he commanded, as if to override the expressions of surprise and concern appearing on the faces of the jurors. Agee, wary of the approaching marshal, began helping Mayo to his feet. The marshal paused and looked at the judge, uncertain whether his services would be needed to restore order.

"That's all right, Mr. Marshal," said Fazio as Mayo regained his full height. The marshal retreated to his position by the door, the ripple of uncertainty that had swept through the jury box faded, and Fazio resumed his questioning. When it was over, Juror 1642 had uttered the word "guilty" five times, looking directly at Mayo the entire time.

Fazio thanked the jurors for their work and dismissed them. After the last juror left, he swept his hand through his hair, nodded his head a couple of times to no one in particular, and proceeded to wrap things up. "In light of the jury's verdict the court will order him detained until sentencing. I'll set a date when I get the pre-sentence report. Very well, if there is nothing else, Mr. Mayo, please step back with the marshal, sir."

"Step back" was of course a euphemism. The marshal escorted Mayo out of the courtroom as Agee watched and McCallum gathered his files.

"Thank you for your work, gentlemen," said Fazio. "This Court will now take a thirty-minute recess."

On cue, Miss Jackson said "All rise," and the attorneys struggled to their feet as Fazio made his exit. McCallum, already packed and ready to leave, crossed the aisle between the lawyers' tables and extended his hand for a hearty parting handshake, as if they'd just played tennis.

Agee let his hand be pumped, and McCallum layered the act with the words "Tough luck. Nice trial." Then he turned and walked briskly out of the room.

Agee's mind was a black hole. He stood there, unable to extract a thought from the silence. The event seemed to be over, but he didn't know what to do next. Eventually, he sat down.

"Counsel, you might want to pay your client a visit before they take him back on the bus," offered Miss Jackson in a surprisingly careful voice. "I'd give him a moment alone though."

"Right," Agee said. He continued to sit. The courtroom looked the same, but he felt like he'd survived an explosion and should be surrounded by rubble.

"Well, you did what you could for him," Miss Jackson said. "Matter of fact, you did a lot better than most of the lawyers we appoint in these cases." There was a pause, then she added, "But if I were you, I'd practice up on a few misdemeanors before taking on another felony. These kids ... these kids got a lot at stake."

Agee nodded dully, but the words cut like a knife.

Miss Jackson straightened her files in the silence, then rose and crossed toward the door. Agee snuck a look at her as she neared the exit, and was surprised by what he saw.

Her eyes seemed wet. He wondered if she had teared up at the verdict.

Agee decided to give Mayo the moment she'd suggested, but needed his own moment first. Then he composed himself and made his way back to the holding cell. This time Mayo was sitting on the steel bench in the back of the cell, eyes closed, hands on his chin, elbows on his legs. A picture of repose except for the streaks across his face where moments before he'd wiped away tears. He got up as soon as Agee entered, and stood close to the bars.

"I'm sorry," Agee said.

Mayo shook his head slowly before replying. "How much time am I gonna to have to do?" he asked.

"I—I don't know," Agee responded, unprepared for the question and searching for an answer that wouldn't make things worse.

"You don't know," repeated Mayo, as if trying to understand how that could be. There was a pause, during which Mayo's eyes found the floor again and Agee noticed how tightly his client's brown hands grasped the steel bars. Then Mayo raised his head and looked at him with an intensity he had not seen before.

"And I thought you was gonna do me right," he said.

"I'm sorry. I thought I was, too" replied Agee.

After that there was nothing else to say, so the two men simply stood there, on either side of the bars, lost in their own thoughts.

In the stillness of the moment, it dawned on Agee how petty his bruised-ego lawyer agonies had been compared to what Mayo had been going through—and what the young man would suffer in the future. What did his worry about some courtroom rite of passage amount to, compared to Mayo's passage to manhood, which was about to be permanently derailed? Yes, he might have to chain-smoke his way through a few days, but then the odds of Mayo being brutalized in the Big House were increasing by the minute. This blunt thought sent a series of images jump-cutting through Agee's mind, random but vivid: a dog curled and bleeding in the snow, Mayo's mother in a shawl, a child sitting on Mayo's stoop.

Agee started to say "Try to hang in there" but he couldn't handle the phrase, even after the images fled his head, so he just said "See you at the jail" and turned away.

"Tell my mom, OK?" asked Mayo, and Agee swallowed and cleared his throat and said, "I will" before leaving.

As he walked back through the courtroom, his left shoe began making an annoying squeaking noise. He cursed, then kicked the wooden base of the witness stand with his foot. Then he kicked it again, harder. As he continued on toward counsel table, he found himself wondering how many defendants like Mayo Miss Jackson had seen. For a second he saw a roller-coaster car filled with them, roaring down the looping tracks, a million Mayos laughing with delight, all seeking the same happy end.

Agee packed his briefcase and left the courtroom. He walked down the crowded hallway alone. Soon he passed the library and came to the marble stairway leading to the main floor of the building. He was just nearing the exit when the phrase "a vast cavern wherein discord wails" sailed into his head for the first time since his college days. At first it seemed just right, an apt metaphor for the Superior Court itself, a perfect objective correlative for Soren Kierkegaard's philosophical take on the universe. Or perhaps it went deeper than that; perhaps it described the new condition of his heart.

But then another thought struck him, hard enough that he stopped and put down his briefcase: the phrase was a message from his soul, or something within him that was struggling to become a soul, and it bore a truth his ego was already trying to hide: Willie Mayo was going to spend a long, long time in a vast cavern called prison, wherein discord surely wailed, and it was Tom Agee's fault. Miss Jackson, he realized, had known all along: pride and inexperience had led him to gamble with a young man's life in an effort to forge a new and exciting career. He'd lost the bet, but his life remained intact. Only Mayo's would be destroyed.

He made his way through a revolving door to a side street where he stood blinking in the afternoon light. Then he remembered he'd left his briefcase in the court building. He pictured it clearly in his mind, sitting on the floor of the hallway he'd just left. He started to go back for it, but stopped after taking a few steps. Then he turned away from the courthouse and walked slowly down the street. His hands were in his pockets, and his eyes sought the ground.

Birds Of A Feather

I'd seen some locked government cases in my time as a defense attorney, but if ever there was a case that cried out for conviction it was United States vs. Marvin Hawkins, a/k/a "The Creeper." I mean, talk about being caught red-handed! Talk about open and shut! It all started when Mr. Hawkins went into a gift shop on the main floor of the Silver Creek Mall the afternoon of December 23. It's the last shopping day before Christmas, the place is packed, and Hawkins sneaks into the back room of The Curio Shop and snatches an envelope containing the day's receipts. So far so good, at least from the career criminal's point of view. But then things go wrong terribly fast. A salesgirl who's been watching the Hawk's attempt to case the joint sees him pick up the envelope and demands he hand it over. Instead, he bolts.

As a seasoned trial lawyer skimming the police report, I immediately think ah-ha, nice move: the crafty felon's going to run out the door, slip into the street traffic, and claim mistaken identity the second they nab him. But Hawkins had a different idea. He ran directly to the closest escalator and tried to escape by riding it to the second floor. Unfortunately that escalator was a down escalator, jam-packed with shoppers trying to claw their way back to the main floor, out of the mall and home for the holidays. There goes the mistaken ID defense, I thought. Was this guy trying to go to jail or what?

In any event there he was, trying to make it up the down escalator, and he may as well have been attempting to break through the front line at Green Bay. And it gets worse. The store clerk yells "Stop, thief!" and as Hawkins jostles the shoppers and gets jostled back, the cash slips out of the stolen envelope and flies in all possible directions. Suddenly, it's bills everywhere! A shower of greenbacks! Crowds of shoppers and uniformed security guards immediately form around each end of the escalator, captivated by the sheer lunatic spectacle of it all.

By the time Hawkins makes his way to the second floor, he is collared, cuffed and slammed to the floor by the only two guards not doubled over with laughter. They read him his rights, collect the money from the helpful, surging crowd ("Officer, please can I be a witness against him? I saw everything!") and ship him to the nearest precinct, where he is booked on every variety of theft known to humankind. Then they cart him to D.C.'s Central Cellblock where, in a stunning move, he denies committing the offense.

I know all this because I was assigned to represent him early the next morning. Right off the bat, during what we defense lawyers like to call the initial client interview, he tries to hit me up for change to make a cellblock phone call to his aunt. I knew right then and there the guy was trouble—there are no pay phones in the cellblock. Later on, I learned he had no aunt. This time, he admitted committing the offense. "Yeah, I took the money," he said. "I'm a Creeper—you know, I creep into offices and stores and take purses and whatever else I can find. But I can't afford to do time for this one. I want a trial."

What a loser, I decided, even before he turned down the prosecutor's first plea offer, leading her to make good on her promise to file repeat offender papers on him. The potential doubling of his sentence didn't rattle Mr. Hawkins, though; he wanted a trial. Why? Simple. He figured he could win.

It's an understatement to say most defense attorneys are zealots willing to go to the wall with their clients, whom they perceive as the ultimate victims of the world: forced to steal, loot, assault and pillage only to feed themselves and their young, and thus deserving of every break in the book. Unfortunates who've been kicked around by life and its darkest manifestation, the court system: abused by judges, overzealous DAs, lying cops and—at times, I'll admit it—ineffective counsel. Not an objective view when you get down to it, but exactly the sort of mentality that's necessary to survive the scorn of the rest of the populace, which asks folks like me at least once a week, "How can you defend those people?" Unchecked, defense attorney zealotry can lead to seven day work weeks, sixteen hour work days, and in extreme cases, requests to install showers in law offices so the lawyers won't lose precious time going home on weekends to clean up.

I bought into it one hundred percent, and why not? In D.C., once you get past the monuments on the Mall, you learn the projects, the prisons, the rehabs *and* the jail cells are filled to the brim with black people and black people only. Seeing that sent me a clear message, so I decided to *fight the power*, as Public Enemy would put it, and defend poor people from my beloved city who were charged with crimes.

And what a fight it's been. Most of the people I represent have never, ever had anyone in their corner. Usually they have no jobs and live at ground zero in the ghetto. Often they are black sheep in their families, troublemakers in school, and terrors in their neighborhoods—people crossed the street to avoid them, even when they were twelve. In short they are pariahs, and when you are a pariah defendant and the assembled forces of justice are mounting a full-scale attack on your liberty, that is exactly when you need someone in your corner—someone who will stand with you, arms linked, while the crowd calls for your blood. Someone like me, in other words, who will *defend* you, not just apologize for you. And I don't mean defend as in try to remain standing while deflecting the spears and arrows; I mean defend by counterattack, with the objective of getting you off scot-free so you can strut your butt out of the courtroom.

In other words, if you're a defendant in a jam, you need me to defend you. I am a put the government on trial, take no prisoners, nail them to the wall defender. Most people don't like me, but I don't care—I'm on a mission. I have an incredible win record—eighty percent of my trials in a city where the government usually wins ninety percent. Why? Because I don't just mouth the standard "Excuse me, I don't want to offend you, I'm just making the government prove its case" rhetoric: I counterpunch the way Ali did with Liston. I don't do this because of any great fealty to the concept of due process of law; I do it for the excitement of combat and the thrill of victory. I want to win cases, not walk defendants to the pen mumbling up my sleeve about how I'd thought we had a good shot.

In short, I'm good, I love my job, and I love my clients no matter how mean, warped and antisocial they are. But even a hardcore trial freak like me had a hard time stomaching Marvin Hawkins. In fact, I wanted to run the other way when I saw him coming. He was usually unkempt, always unshaven, and constantly seeking advantage. His face had a furtive look permanently etched on it, and his slicked-back hair, thin countenance and prominent incisors led me to imagine him with fur and a tail, sneaking down an alleyway looking for something to gnaw on. He was also irritating in countless small ways that built up fast: bumming cigarette change, using the office phone, asking for a ride home, picking up another charge in a neighboring county that he didn't disclose—anything to make life more complicated.

"Mr. Spencer, you think you could let me have ten dollars for a cab ride home? My aunt's sick and I'd like to get home fast. It's a long, long walk in this ninety-degree weather, you know. I bet *you* got a ride home." That sort of thing. In the criminal world, you could get boxed and buried for being that irritating. I began thinking he was lucky to still be alive.

But then it seemed Hawkins also had good luck in making bail pre-trial. The odds of that happening weren't great—he had a couple of convictions, the case against him was strong, and not surprisingly, no one was able to verify his claim that he worked nights distributing newspapers for the local daily. Yet somehow he convinced the judge he was gainfully employed, and even though the DA asked for a five thousand dollar bond, he'd walked out of the courtroom, free to creep on until his trial date.

I noticed fortune seemed to smile on Hawkins in the courtroom as well. Over the years, most of the charges against him wound up being dismissed, and he'd been acquitted after trial in five of the seven remaining cases. At first, I wondered if he got a lot of mileage out of being what I call a Felony Two defendant: someone who commits relatively innocuous theft crimes—steals your purse or your car, shoplifts, winds up with the check in your mailbox, etc. They don't seem so threatening, and compared to the Felony One crew, which is out there day in and day out committing murder and mayhem, they aren't. Felony Twos tend to slip through the cracks—prosecutors dismiss their cases when witnesses don't show, judges tend to grant defense motions more often, the cases get continued until they die. Yet looking at Hawkins' rap sheet, with scores of arrests but only two priors, I began thinking there was more than Felony Two mileage involved. Was it just plain good luck? Did the DAs laugh so hard at his ineptitude that they forgot to prepare their cases? Or was there something else to it?

In any event, Hawkins had skated on occasions when most defendants would fall through the ice and drown. As a result, he pretty much assumed he was invulnerable. He was confident he'd beat the current charges too, even with a bad lawyer. That's right; in addition to irritating the hell out of me, he wasted no time making clear his disappointment with the quality of my lawyering.

Within a week I had reviewed the relevant police reports, sent my investigator to interview the salesgirl at the shop, and tracked down two hostile witnesses—spectators who had taken an instant dislike to Hawkins and jumped at the chance to help put him away. Next I met with "Felony Florence" Merson, the Assistant U.S. Attorney handling the matter. Amused by the Hawk's failed getaway attempt, Merson described him as a living embodiment of the maxim "You don't have to be smart to be a criminal."

She swore she'd never seen such a strong case before, and she was probably right. By the time she'd finished recounting the evidence against Hawkins, I knew the only thing missing was a video of the offense taken by Abraham Zapruder.

Merson, usually no friend of the defense bar, actually took pity on me. But that didn't necessarily translate into a sweet deal for my client.

"Tell you what," she said, "your man's slipped through the cracks before, and since he turned down our initial plea offer, which I considered more than generous, we'll let him plead to the lead count in the indictment and we won't ask for him to be locked up until sentencing."

"That's it?" I asked. "You won't even withdraw the repeat papers? What about the bargain part of the plea bargain?" Merson just laughed—much like I imagined Hawkins' arresting officers had laughed—and told me that was the best she could do.

"What possible defense could you put on," she said, "and don't tell me insanity." But I haggled with her for almost an hour, and she finally agreed to withdraw the repeats. Still not much of a deal, but as Merson reminded me, at least it limited my man's exposure to ten years. "Talk to him," she admonished me as I made for the door, and as much as I hate plea bargains, I said I surely would.

Since Hawkins was out on bail and not burdened by a strong work ethic, it took me a while to catch up with him. I tried setting up meetings in my office, but he didn't show. After two missed appointments, I took to swinging by his mother's house—he lived with his mother, who struck me as a first-class enabler—but he was never there.

"He's out working; he works *so* hard," she always told me, shaking her head with sympathy for her son, yet she never knew where he was, much less his line of work.

Finally he showed up in my office unannounced, the day before I was scheduled to start a murder one trial. Of course he wanted immediate service—that is, right after he used my phone for some personal calls. I did a slow burn until he was done, then began touting the benefits of the plea offer. He looked at me like I was a flatworm.

"Look," I told him, "you have a right to a trial before a jury, true. And if you decide to go to trial, I will defend you to the best of my ability. But the DA is going to march a platoon of witnesses into that courtroom, and when she asks them who did it, they're all going to point at you. Bad judgment is not a legal defense, and you have no other defense I'm aware of. I mean it's not like a drug dealer put a gun to your head and told you to steal the money. Mr. Hawkins, it's in your best interest to cut your losses. My advice is take the plea and limit your exposure to ten years instead of twenty."

In other words I rushed the pitch, largely because I was pressed and he'd taken so much of my time already, and he felt I was railroading him. "Mr. Spencer," he whined, "I been in jail before and I'm not going back. I got a lot on my mind. If it comes down to it, I might not even show up for the trial." I told him that if he didn't show, he'd pick up a free failure to appear charge worth five years in any prison, and besides he'd only be buying a few weeks before the marshals came to get him. He didn't say anything, and I thought I could see him weighing the possibilities. But I was wrong—he had something else on his mind.

"It's hard for me to think right now, bein' as I'm so hungry," he said finally, eyeing the carryout bag on my desk. "You got a sandwich or somethin' in there you can spare for a hungry man?" I was starving and if he hadn't shown up I would have been eating, but I lifted my ham and Swiss out of the bag and gave it to him. He took his time eating it, and didn't seem inclined to talk while he chewed, so I left the office for a few minutes and ran record checks on witnesses in my murder case.

When I came back, I saw he'd helped himself to my soda and the rest of my lunch as well. The man had no shame. "So what do you think, Mr. Hawkins?" I asked, surreptitiously checking to see that nothing worth selling had disappeared from my desk. I was relieved to note that the solid gold pen set a former client had given me after his acquittal was still there. "You want to think about it a while?"

"OK, let me ask you," he replied, wiping his mouth slowly with a napkin yet missing the specks of cheese on his lower lip. "When you said before about the drug dealer putting a gun to my head, you were saying that would be a defense, right?" I sensed where this was going, and moved quickly to stop it.

"Look. It would be a defense if that's what happened, but we know it *didn't* happen, and I can't—"

"What do you mean, we know it didn't happen?" he interrupted.

"Oh no you don't, Mr. Hawkins," I countered. "You told me you took the cash. You said the risk of creeping was you got caught sometimes, and this was one of those times. Remember saying that?"

He didn't miss a beat. "Well, see when I told you that I left some things out. That's because at that time I didn't trust you. On account of I've had some bad lawyers before, and we'd just met and as you know it takes some time for a lawyer and client to develop a relationship of trust."

The ham and cheese must have inspired him—I guess it took a free meal to get his creative juices flowing. "So? Where are you going with this?" I asked, fondling the aspirin tin in my drawer.

"So because I didn't trust you," he replied, "I left out the part about the drug dealer."

"Let me get this straight. You never mentioned anything about a drug dealer before. But now, because you suddenly trust me, you want to tell me... what? That some drug dealer put a gun to your head and forced you to commit the crime?"

At this point I was ready to prosecute him myself. I was also visibly upset, something he seemed to enjoy.

"Well, like if a drug dealer who I owed money to told me, 'You get that money to me in half an hour or I'm gonna kill you,' would that be a defense?"

"Depends on the facts," I said, still hoping to head him off. "You're talking about a duress defense, which is extremely hard to mount."

"That's OK," he replied, "Nothin' like a challenge. But maybe I'll wait a while before I reveal the rest of the facts to you."

I'd had enough Hawkins for one sitting. "Look, the trial's still a month away," I said abruptly. "It would be good if you could tell me the rest of what happened sometime before it starts. Meanwhile, I'll call the DA and tell her you nixed the plea offer. Now if you'll excuse me, I have to get ready for a murder trial."

"I bet your defendant in the murder is a drug dealer just like the one who duressed me," he said ungrammatically as he rose from his chair. I looked to see if there was a tail between his legs—but at that moment, there wasn't.

"You know, the jury's not going to like hearing you got in this jam in the first place because of your involvement in the drug trade."

"We'll just have to go where the truth takes us," he replied as he got up to leave, "but I'll think about that."

* * *

I saw him again after the murder trial. The jury had hung, I was exhausted, and in walks Hawkins with a dog-eared copy of *Perkins On Criminal Law* under his arm.

"I borrowed this from a used book store for a while," he intoned, smiling at me. Many defendants like to do legal research, either out of curiosity or as a check on their attorneys, so this didn't bother me at first. But then Hawkins put the book on my desk and began reading from a passage he'd underlined with a lime-green highlighter: "Compulsion which will excuse the commission of a crime must be present, imminent, and impending, and of such a nature as to induce a well-grounded apprehension of death or great bodily harm if the act is not done," he declared.

"Tell me more," I said, biting down on my dislike for the man. After all, I reminded myself, he's a client.

"Attorney Spencer, you tole me it was duress but according to *Perkins On Criminal Law* it's also called compulsion," he noted with an air of superiority. "I'm gonna leave this book here so you can look it over."

"A little legal research can be a dangerous thing," I replied, still biting down. He shook his head, as if to chastise me for my lack of faith, before continuing.

"Now, about this here drug dealer I mentioned last time. See, I owed him money and he said if I didn't get it to him in half an hour he was gonna kill me. He was right nearby and he had a gun and I *truly* believed and apprehended that if I didn't rob that shop then and there to get that money he was gonna kill me just like he said."

I'd been taught the best way to disabuse a defendant of a dumb scheme was not to argue the morality of it, but instead show him how, as a practical matter, it would blow up in his face.

"Look," I began. "What drug dealer? There's no evidence on the planet that supports what you're trying to say. None. All we can do is put you on the stand to tell your—your *story*, and then pow!—the DA is going to roll out your record and the jury is going to convict you in minutes. The Phantom Drug Dealer Defense. Great."

My tirade seemed to give him pause. He reflected, wiped a bubble of saliva off his lip, and reflected some more.

"You see Mister Spencer," he said finally—and at this point a condescending tone began seeping into his voice—"if you was a drug dealer and you told me to get you the money and you saw I got arrested tryin' to get that very same money to pay you, would you stick around?"

I could see this guy was going to be a problem every inch of the way. "All right, Mr. Hawkins. Fine. What's this supposed drug dealer's name?" I demanded.

"I can't tell you that for the same reason I couldn't say no when he told me to steal the money," he said, not missing a beat.

He was practiced, man. He'd been born lying.

"It's just like you was saying. No one in his right mind would go into a store loaded with people like that, on a busy shopping day, and try to steal something in broad daylight. Unless someone put a gun to his head and told him to do it."

I fell silent. At this point I knew, deep down in my heart, that unless the store went bankrupt and its owners disappeared without a trace, we were going to trial. This despite the fact that everything about the guy—his furtive-looking face, his criminal record, his previous fabrications—told me he was lying through his nicotine-stained teeth.

"And where was this nameless drug dealer waiting for you to deliver the goods?" I asked.

There was another pause, while he ran the next falsehood through his mind to see if it held water. Evidently he concluded it did: "Attorney Spencer, you know he had to be waiting on the second floor, right at the top of that escalator. That's where he told me he would be. Or else why on earth would I try and run up the down escalator in traffic like that?"

Why else indeed. "Don't you *see*," I railed, "the prosecutor is going to say you made up this incredible story because you were caught red handed and there isn't anything else you could possibly come up with."

"I know that," he replied, beginning to show some real exasperation. "And *I'm* going to say I had to do it because the drug dealer told me he'd shoot me if I didn't. In other words, two different virgins of what happened, and the only way to resolve the matter is to have us a trial."

"Mr. Hawkins," I continued, now massaging my temples, "I am what they call an officer of the court. As such, I am not allowed to lie to the court, and I am not allowed to put a witness on the stand who I know is going to lie to the court."

"So, how do you know I'm lying? Are you God?"

"No," I admitted.

"Don't I have a right to put on a defense? I'm an innocent man, an innocent man who's being railroaded, and I need good legal counsel."

The scary thing was the way he said it. He actually sounded like an innocent man who was telling the truth. I sat there in shock for a moment, knowing things were spinning out of control but not sure where they'd land.

"Mr. Spencer," he continued, "I'm just asking you for legal advice. That's your job, isn't it, to give people like me legal advice? If you can't do that, maybe I need to get another lawyer."

I could see the scenario even as he rehearsed it in his mind: wait until the next court date, then ask for a new lawyer, who would of course need more time to prepare for trial, and so on until the case died of old age. I decided to cut him off at the pass, and told him the judge wouldn't replace me because I had a great win-loss record and was well respected around the courthouse.

"OK then," he said, backtracking seamlessly. "Now, these days, the defense is usually called 'duress,' isn't it?"

"It is, and if you assert that defense and lose, you are going to be under duress for up to twenty years, Mr. Hawkins."

"But I won't lose," he replied. "I got me a fine lawyer. I just heard all about your win-loss record. You're just the one to convince the jury I was a desperate man, forced to commit the act against my will on account of death threats from this here drug dealer."

We just looked at each other, then he flashed his yellow-toothed smile. He knew he had me. "He was really a terrifying sight," he added. "I can describe him if you like."

By that point there was nothing to do but prepare for trial. I didn't believe him, but as he had pointed out my job was to defend him, not judge him. I set up a meeting with him later in the week, by which time I hoped my anger would be in remission. As he left, Hawkins paused in the hallway, then popped his favorite question. "You got any change you could give me for the bus?"

I couldn't help myself. "Sorry," I replied, "I spent my all my cash on your lunch. Maybe you'll run into a drug dealer somewhere who'll force you to steal a bus." He gave me his wounded look, then turned and made his way down the hallway. I kept my eyes on him until he left the building, because I knew full well that if he passed an empty office with an open door, he'd enter it.

I was in my office a week later preparing another case when I grasped the real reason why Hawkins' visit had left me vibrating like a tuning fork. The words *Lies Like Truth*, the title of a book by Harold Clurman resting on my bookshelf, leapt out at me. Clurman was not a brilliant lawyer who wrote about trial preparation. Au contraire, he was a brilliant theater director who wrote about acting.

I had read the book because like many trial lawyers, I'd taken some acting classes in my neophyte days, hoping to impress jurors with the kind of stage presence good actors have. In the course of a series of classes with egomaniacal drama teachers, I learned that really good actors didn't think of themselves as acting at all. They didn't "pretend" to be their characters. Instead, they developed a technique that allowed them to change the text and the situation they were working with—fictions both—into something their inner selves accepted as "real" —and thus transform their "performances" into something truthful and authentic.

Basically, you took the facts in the fiction (we're in a house in Pittsburg; I'm an ex-con former baseball player named Troy who is fighting with his son) and ran them through your imagination in great detail, "seeing" them in your mind's eye again and again until they took on the same reality—as far as your body's storehouse of memories was concerned—as authentic memories of your actual experiences. It was like seeing a movie in your mind and replaying it until your body accepted it as real. If you succeeded, it meant that when you uttered a line by August Wilson or Lorraine Hansberry, it read as if you had actually lived through the experience you were recounting. In that sense, you were weaving a "lie like truth."

The greatest actors had always been able to do this, the gurus told me; some achieved it through rigorous training with gifted teachers, but others did it instinctively. Of course I saw the potential for this sort of process to transform my closing arguments—in fact, all my courtroom behavior before juries—into dramatic moments cloaked in an aura of truth and authenticity. I worked hard to master the technique and by this point had used it in the courtroom with great success for many years. As I pled my case, it would read to the jury as if I had actually witnessed my client's version of the facts and was recounting real experience to them. They would be convinced of the truthfulness of what I said, and acquit my client forthwith.

But now I realized what I was dealing with in the Curio Shop case. Hawkins, I decided, was intuitively a great actor. He may have been a sneak and a mooch and a failed felon, incapable of leaving a crime scene without wearing cuffs, but he clearly had the great actor's ability to engage his imagination at will and transform his lies into something that seemed like truth.

Despite my newfound respect for Hawkins' acting ability, I found it hard to mount the energy needed to prepare for his trial. This upset me—he was facing a lot of time and it was inconsistent with my self-image as the *Uber*-defender. Still, I wasn't motivated. I resorted to asking colleagues to help prepare the defense. I showed them the passage Hawkins had highlighted in *Perkins*, explained he was serious about the duress defense, and had them cross-examine him the way I expected Merson to go at him. I expected my fellow lawyers would trip him up, but no dice: he stuck to his story and, as incredible as that story was, managed to make it sound convincing each time out.

Still, I expected the trial to be a disaster. I knew Felony Florence would press Hawkins to reveal the name of the drug dealer who had allegedly coerced him into committing the theft, and that when he demurred the judge would order him to answer the question. He'd have to answer, I told him, because he'd be waiving his Fifth Amendment right to remain silent by taking the stand. And if he made up a name, they would run a record check, come up with zero and catch him in the lie. Nevertheless, the Hawk stuck with his earlier response: "I can't tell you the man's name because if I do he'll kill me."

I advised him, in no uncertain terms, that when he was ordered to reveal the dealer's name at trial the defense would fall apart. He simply smiled and said, "I'll give the matter some thought."

In true Hawkins fashion, he showed up late for the trial, entering the courtroom just as the judge was about to issue a warrant for his arrest. But within minutes he convinced the judge that a bizarre series of Metrobus-related events had conspired to delay his arrival. His tardiness was excused and a jury panel was summoned for voir dire. I assumed the bus story was a total fabrication, and that Hawkins had used it to warm up for his big performance.

The first half of the trial, up until Hawkins' direct examination, didn't go very well. I was off. I found it hard to focus. I didn't seem able to summon up the empathy I needed to defend the man successfully. True, there was little I could do with the parade of solid citizen witnesses who recounted every detail of Hawkins' bungled criminal adventure for the jury. But their testimony didn't kill us, because it was consistent with our defense—which admitted he committed the crime, but contended the act should be excused under the law. I stumbled through my opening but managed to tell the jury that "at first, this case will appear simple to you, like the government says. But please, keep an open mind until Mr. Hawkins testifies, and then listen very carefully to what he has to say. If you do, you will learn there is far more to this case than what meets the eye." This admonition served to make the jury wary of what was actually an airtight case, and kept us afloat, despite my lackluster performance, until the government rested.

Then it was our turn. Luckily for the defense, Hawkins had cleaned up his act for the trial; he was clean-shaven and actually wore the tie I'd loaned him. Even better, he did unbelievably well on direct examination: he was convincing, he was believable, he was the Brando of the courtroom. Clearly, it seemed, a drug dealer had forced him to steal the money from the shop. But as I knew, cross-examination lay before him like a minefield.

"Mister Hawkins," said Merson, cutting to the chase with her first question, "you claim that a drug dealer made you steal the money. And what, pray tell, was the name of that drug dealer?" My client didn't reply, so Merson piled on: "You know, the dealer who left no trace of his existence behind?"

There was a hush in the courtroom, as Hawkins finally said, in a low voice suddenly tinged with fear, "I'd rather not give his name, if you don't mind, because . . . I'm afraid of what he might do to me if . . . you know."

This too seemed eminently believable—I could even see jurors getting peeved at Merson for putting the poor Mr. Hawkins in this predicament—but the prosecutor forged ahead, unleashing a barrage of questions designed to force Hawkins to reveal the dealer's name. Finally, faced with the defendant's unrelenting refusal to give up the name, Merson got the judge to order him to disclose it.

There followed a moment of silence, which Hawkins milked for all it was worth before lowering his head and uttering the barely audible words "Francis Coulter."

Then, most predictably, Merson unleashed a volley of follow-up questions about "this so-called Coulter," designed to show the jury Hawkins had pulled the name out of thin air. Where did he live? Hawkins gave an address, and I shuddered. How old was he? Hawkins said he was 32 or 33 and that they had gone to high school together. I shuddered again. "What high school?" Merson asked, barely containing her joy as she led the defendant down the garden path, eliciting a series of answers she knew she could prove false.

Indeed Hawkins answered every question in great detail, and soon Merson had elicited from him the complete life story of Francis Coulter. I was not surprised when she asked for a recess so the government could look further into the Coulter matter. I knew Felony Florence planned to run address and record checks during the break, and return to the courtroom armed with documentation that would prove beyond a doubt Hawkins had lied like a fox.

Of course I too was hearing the Coulter story for the first time, so I checked around during the recess as well. I was stunned to discover that a Francis Coulter lived at the very address supplied by Hawkins. Not only that, he lived in Hawkins' neighborhood and even had a record that suggested he was a drug dealer! My investigator soon confirmed that Coulter had gone to the same high school as Hawkins. Much to my surprise, I caught myself wondering for a second whether Hawkins was telling the truth. Then I decided Francis Coulter was someone he really knew, and that he'd simply borrowed him as the source for the "factual" information he'd revealed on cross. Perhaps he was even making an effort to draw Coulter into the trial—to get the DA to put the man on the stand to deny everything, so that when he did, I could argue to the jury that they should believe Hawkins rather than Coulter, and acquit. Either way, I realized, Hawkins had taken control of the defense. Perhaps that was for the best.

Once Merson learned there was a real-life Coulter, she wasted no time asking the judge for another recess to find the man and get him on the stand to deny everything Hawkins had said. The judge granted a one-hour recess, during which I paced nervously in the hallway until Hawkins took my arm and said, "Don't worry about it, Mr. Spencer. They ain't gonna get that man in the courtroom." I wasn't so sure.

Soon we were summoned into the courtroom, where at the bench, a crestfallen Merson told the judge that while there was a Coulter and the police had been able to document everything Hawkins said about him, the man was recently deceased. It seemed that Coulter had been hit by a car a little over a week ago. He'd lingered awhile in intensive care before becoming permanently unavailable for trial.

I knew then that we had a shot if I could muster up the skill. My task would be to argue the corroboration between Hawkins' testimony and the facts, regret Coulter's untimely death, and point out that Hawkins was unaware of said untimely death when he testified, which made his testimony even more credible. I began to think that if I could render effective assistance of counsel, my client might walk out of the courtroom to resume his life of crime after all.

But Merson, career prosecutor that she was, had a different view: she figured Hawkins knew all along that Coulter was dead, and since dead men tell no tales, would not be around to contradict his sworn testimony. Soon we were back in action, and Merson wasted no time making that very point: "Of course, as you were sitting here this morning telling the jury all about how Francis Coulter threatened to kill you if you didn't come up with the money you owed him, you knew all along that he was DEAD, didn't you?" She was pumped up and trying her best to convey a sense of roaring moral outrage, but the jury barely noticed her.

Instead, they watched transfixed as Hawkins dropped his jaw in amazement. "Dead?" he repeated, quite evidently stunned. "Oh my god. I mean, Francis threatened to kill me and all, but . . . somehow under everything we were still . . . because on the street . . . he just had to do . . . what he had to do . . . if . . . if you know what I mean."

For a second Hawkins stared into the middle distance. He seemed shocked, unnerved, dazed. Then he sighed and said simply but compellingly, "I am so sorry to hear that." You could have heard a pin drop—it was the tragedy of the streets personified. Even Merson was yanked out of her "outraged prosecutor" role and touched by the raw electric moment: we had all watched a man learn for the first time that his childhood friend had died, and react to it with shock and sadness. After that, nothing else seemed to matter. Who cared any more if this was a trial about theft of property from a curio shop, after seeing a bomb like this blow up in the poor man's face?

But I was the person most affected by Hawkins' response. *My God*, I thought—*he's been telling the truth all along!* Suddenly, everything he'd been telling me began fitting together, and I realized to my chagrin that because of my intense dislike for the man I hadn't fulfilled my basic obligation to him as a defense lawyer. So what if he was a walking irritation, he still had constitutional rights, didn't he? Didn't Darrow have a sign on his door that read "We Defend Everyone?" Everyone—not just people we liked. I may as well have been another prosecutor, I told myself, so sure had I been that my client was fabricating his entire defense. No, Hawkins wasn't a liar blessed with an actor's imagination—he was simply a client who'd tried his best, in his aggravating way, to get me to defend him the way I was supposed to. After realizing this and cursing myself for it, I vowed I'd make amends in what remained of the trial.

The passion that had thus far been missing from my defense soon began to manifest itself, and things began looking better and better for us. It helped that Merson never got back in the saddle again. She stumbled through her questions, and even as she faltered Hawkins seemed to extend himself to her, as if making a noble effort to help the proceedings along even as he grieved. Merson and the government were done for if I could rise to the occasion in closing argument.

And rise I did. Raw emotion coursed through my veins as I painted a picture for the jury of what had really happened—a most vivid picture of Coulter's threats, of Coulter's loaded steel-gray Magnum, of how Mr. Hawkins did what any one of us would have done in that situation to stay alive. Using the acting techniques I had developed over the years, I orchestrated the argument perfectly. My words and images vibrated once again with the ring of truth. To cap it off, I recreated the moment during Hawkins' testimony when he realized Coulter was dead. By the end, I had to fight back tears as I urged the jury to go to the jury room and do justice.

Merson practically did a war dance in rebuttal, but the jury wasted little time returning a Not Guilty verdict.

I shook hands with Hawkins after the verdict and apologized for misjudging him. He said, "No problem, Attorney Spencer. I understand. 'Cause I've been misunderstood all my life." He thanked me for my services and told me that "Underneath it all, you know, you and me are birds of a feather."

I wasn't sure what he meant by that, but before I could explore the matter, he smiled and asked me if I would mind paying for his taxi ride home; his mother was sick and he wanted to get back right away and tell her the news. I smiled too, but didn't chastise him this time. Instead, I gave him a ten-spot. Then, after telling him I planned to spend my next ten dollars at Mike's Lounge across the street, I wished him well and excused myself.

I left the courtroom in a hurry, eager to be by myself and compose my thoughts. Maybe it was time for a sabbatical, I thought, as I made my way through the courthouse and across the street for a drink and some self-reflection.

A jury trial is a great thing, I remember thinking as I made my way back to the office an hour later. It's so easy to misjudge a person, to make the wrong judgment based on less than a full picture—but somehow the truth always surfaces during a trial. As I made my way down the hallway, my fellow lawyers congratulated me on yet another not guilty verdict. After a hearty round of handshakes and hugs, I got to my door. I noticed it was ajar and braced myself to find another client waiting inside for my services.

The room was empty, but someone had taken a manila envelope from the stack of mail in my in-box and placed it front and center on my desk. I opened it and saw it contained an obituary notice for one Francis Coulter. It had been cut from the back pages of the local newspaper and was dated a week before the trial. The factual information in it had been underlined carefully with a lime-green highlighter. The kicker was, the package had been mailed the same day the obit appeared in the paper.

I stood there, feeling my cheeks turning red, pondering again what a slippery thing the truth was. He'd been brilliant, absolutely brilliant—and guilty as hell. "Lies like truth," I said to myself, "lies like truth." For a second I entertained the notion that one of my colleagues had engineered a practical joke while I was at Mike's, knowing Hawkins had underlined the passage in *Perkins* using a lime-green marker. It was a comforting thought. But then I noticed my gold pen set was missing from my desk.

Fresh Eyes

The summer of 2001 was even hotter than the one before it. The D.C. body count was rising too, rising so fast Angie thought it might hit three hundred by August. But at the moment, the crime wave was something that concerned her only as a citizen of the District, not as a practitioner in the city's criminal justice system.

She thought back on the year. She and James had gone to the Virgin Islands in the fall, after she got out of rehab. They'd spent a month on the beaches, relaxing. Not drinking. He'd been good about not drinking when she was around, and she had been good about not drinking when he wasn't around.

After the Islands, they visited her parents before returning to D.C. She'd taught a class on criminal justice issues for the Bar—no, not *that* bar, she joked to herself—and he continued to build his practice. Throughout the spring she'd kept herself busy drafting appeals and doing legal research for a small firm. But it wasn't nearly enough.

Her suspension had ended in the spring, so she'd been eligible to practice law for three months now. She wanted to get back into it, but wasn't sure if handling criminal cases again was the best path forward. It was what she longed to do—and had done for years, as a public defender and then as a solo practitioner, until the stress got to her. It had seeped into her system, felony by felony, and she turned to drink to stave it off.

Now she was back in calmer waters, relaxing, eating well, practicing yoga. Even taking a course on French Impressionism at the Smithsonian. But she also felt caught in a velvet vise of her own making: penned in between a regimen of protective self-care and the resulting life of soul-destroying boredom. Weeks ago, she'd decided she could stand some excitement every now and then without becoming a stumbling drunk again. The truth was, she missed trial work.

Do not get lamebrain sentimental about this stuff, she ordered herself. *You haven't tried a case in ages. Your life is different now; you're off the sauce, you have responsibilities, you have a lover. Give yourself one pea-brained reason not to do this and that will be enough.*

But no such reason leapt into her consciousness.

Still, she'd surprised herself when she decided to ring up Kadisha Day, her former Public Defender Service trial chief, after all this time. They caught up for a while, sticking to neutral news, until Kadisha asked her if she was "doing well." That was a polite way to put it, and Angie appreciated it. But it was time to be frank, not feckless, even with her old friend. Sooner or later, everyone wanted the update on an alcoholic. She understood why, so she laid it out up front: she was thinking about practicing again. She went on to confess it had been over a year since she'd been allowed in court, so she was a little rusty. She even admitted her shrink wasn't sure she should take on the tension that came with the territory.

"So the easy thing would be, avoid the déjà vu, and find something else to do. But frankly Miss K, I miss the whole thing, and I was wondering about taking on a starter case—not a Felony I or anything big-time," she rushed to add, "but something that would give me a chance to help someone out and get before a jury before I die of boredom."

"You serious?" was Kadisha's instant response.

"I am, yes. I can handle some of the less fun-filled aspects of life here and there now; I'm ready for that. More than ready, actually. I guess you don't think it's a good idea?"

Day was silent for a good stretch of time, long enough for Angie to ask if she was still on the line.

"I'm here, just . . . thinking what a great run you had. Enough high stakes for a lifetime, but look what it did to you."

"Yes, I know, and yes, it was my fault. Thought I was invincible. Clarence Darrow with a skirt on. Took on way too much."

"You were too—passionate, about your cases."

"Well, you have to be. Comes with the territory."

"True. To a degree."

"So what do you think, K?"

"Yeah. I was about to say, maybe it's . . . ."

"K, listen, I've been going to AA meetings three times a week. Haven't touched the stuff since they suspended me. So far so good. So I'm thinking a few cases here and there, no huge caseload, no eight days a week. I'd actually like that. Plus maybe keep a few young men out of prison in the bargain . . . . You smoking cigarettes?"

"No, that was a sigh. Angie, if you think you're ready—really really ready—there's a co-defendant case we have to conflict out of. Armed robbery gun. We already represent one of them, so we can't keep the one Judge Stern just assigned to us."

Angie's chest tightened and her heart leapt. "You know anything about the case?"

"Only that it was a street robbery. One of them pulled a thirty-eight and they took the victim's purse. Allegedly."

"Sounds like a good starter case."

"Angie, armed robbery is still a potential life offense. So the stakes are high for this kid, which means they'll be high for you. You know how you get."

"I'm not like that any more. Hey, I'm sipping black coffee, even as we speak."

"Well—he's eighteen and doesn't have a record."

"Fresh meat for the system. I'd like to maybe talk to the kid, see how it goes."

"Your call, Ang—seriously. But if you want the case, check in with Judge Stern's chambers and let them know. It'll be his call."

"I'll do that. Right, see what he says. I mean I think I'm ready. What's making me anxious is time is passing and I— the longer I wait . . . you know."

Kadisha said she knew, repeated her "make sure you're ready" advice, and got off the phone with the "I have to run, I'll call you later" exit line Angie had become accustomed to.

* * *

As it turned out, Stern wanted to meet with her in person before letting her take the case. It made sense. He wanted to make sure she was off the booze and able to stay off it before taking on a job that had consequences for others. That was good; it meant he wanted the defendant to be well represented. There were a few judges, she remembered, who made a practice of appointing the worst defense attorneys to the most serious cases. Long-range planning for a conviction. Prosecutors in robes, essentially.

Stern said she should meet with the defendant, see how

it felt, and if she was comfortable representing him to call chambers and he'd appoint her to the case. She had to promise to let him know if she faltered, or was struggling with it at all, so he could get her help—and get the defendant another attorney. Not exactly a vote of confidence, but she was learning to live with the carefully phrased doubts of others. The smart thing to do would be to move to another state. Start fresh, she thought for a moment. But like her former clients used to tell her, the past has a way of tracking you down. So best to make a stand here.

After Stern finished checking her out, they shook hands and he wished her good luck. "Here's to a fresh start," he said. "And that's not a toast."

"Great sense of humor, judge." She rolled her eyes, and he shrugged. "Thanks for the second chance."

* * *

She called the kid's number later that day, but the line was disconnected—some things never changed. He was due back in court in a week for a status hearing, so she wanted to see him right away. It was already late afternoon, and she didn't want to be caught across the river after dark, so within the hour she was pumping the foot pedal on her Jetta, coaxing its fickle engine to start. Half an hour later she was on the Southeast Freeway, racing over the listless Anacostia River toward Martin Luther King Avenue.

Soon she was in her old stomping grounds, remembering moments from past cases as she cruised through familiar neighborhoods. Alabama Avenue, then Fort Dupont Park—amazing, how little the Fort had changed. She wondered whose turf it was now. She looped up to East Capitol Street, passing one crime-ridden neighborhood after another along the way: Benning Heights, Glendale, then Capitol View and the 50s, a few short blocks away from 56th Street, where the kid lived.

The side streets still didn't look inviting. The houses were set apart, but she'd forgotten how tiny they looked. As if they'd been built on a smaller scale to fit the needs of a lesser people. There were Projects here and there too: grim, standard-issue brick buildings replete with iron bars and graffiti. She'd seen it all before, but now she was seeing it with fresh eyes and it stung.

A few minutes later she was in the 400 block of 56th Street, cruising the blacktop slowly, air conditioner on high, looking for a door with the number 442 on it. Four-thirty in the afternoon, but there wasn't much going on. No children in the playground or the weed-filled vacant lots nearby, no adults lounging in lawn chairs or sitting on stoops. Just a few time-tested cars parked on the street or rusting in dirt driveways. All in all, the block seemed eerily empty given the time of day.

Then she saw the house. Number 442 was a small square dwelling with a chain-link fence surrounding its front yard. It was painted white with high-gloss brown trim around the door and windows, and appeared to be propped up on all four corners by stacks of cement blocks—an architectural choice one wouldn't find on the other side of the river.

Her stomach tightened, but at the same time she felt a trace of emotion, a tug on her gut: it was like she was going home again.

She got out of the Jetta and scanned the street, but saw nothing that gave her pause. She chirped the lock and walked through the fence gate and up to the front door. Rang the doorbell, waited, and rang again.

"*Come on*," she demanded. "I'm sweating to death out here."

"Who's there?" asked a female voice from within.

"Hi, I'm Angela Donald. I called before about Jermaine's case, but the line was out," she replied. "I'm an attorney."

She stood in the heat, perspiring, and counted the number of locks being opened. Iron bars disengaged. Beads of sweat dribbled down her face and neck. She felt thirsty.

The door opened, revealing a brown-skinned woman who looked to be about forty and was likely Jermaine's mother or aunt. The woman looked drawn and worried and Angie's anger receded the moment she saw her. She invited Angie into a living room that was dimly lit, the window shades having been drawn down in a failed effort to ward off the heat. The shades were so thin a soft, yellow-gold light floated through them and spilled across the barely furnished room.

She noted there was no scent of alcohol, then scolded herself for thinking there might be.

"I'm his mother," said the woman. "June. Excuse me I got to lock the door again; I'll jus' do the bolt and the chain. You never know 'round here, even in daylight."

After June finished with the door she turned to Angie and said, "You can have a seat there on the couch. I'll get Jermaine."

She cut through a small kitchenette to a back room and emerged a minute later with a tall, lanky young man wearing jeans and a T-shirt with the words *Air Jordan* stenciled across its front. *A hero? Let's hope so*, Angie thought.

"This Jermaine. Say hello, Jermaine."

"Hello."

"Hi, Jermaine." Angie moved closer to the teen, who looked barely old enough to be charged as an adult. "I'm

Angela Donald; good to meet you." She offered her hand and he extended his and shook it. It was the soft, awkward handshake kids his age tended to give.

"Listen, I got a call from the Public Defender Service. They can't keep your case because someone in their office represents the other person charged with the robbery."

His eyes darted over to his mother and then back to her.

"Yeah, but see—I don't got the money to hire a pay lawyer."

"You wouldn't have to pay me a fee."

"OK . . . so, what, you're gonna take over my case?"

"Well, we should talk about a few things first. Here's my card—can I see your court papers?" She gave him one of the cards she'd had printed before the suspension.

"Yeah. I guess."

June bristled. "Don't say yeah, say 'yes ma'am,' Jermaine."

"*OK . . . Yes ma'am.*"

He handed her the stenciled release papers he'd been given at arraignment. She skimmed them while he read the card.

"You have to go to court next Thursday. Nine o'clock sharp."

"What's gonna happen? The trial?"

"No—they call it a status hearing. The judge'll check on the case, maybe set a trial date. Make sure you're on time Thursday, though."

The kid put his hands on his hips and stared at the floor and said "Yeah."

"You have a way to get to court?"

"Forty-two bus."

"Great."

There was a silence. It occurred to her the two of them

might be thinking their lives weren't worth all that much in the grand scheme of things. It was a notion she didn't want to become part of their makeup. To bore into their minds, bit by bit, like some soul-killing worm. She'd seen it happen before.

It was time to ramp things up a bit.

"Jermaine I want to tell you something: as a defense attorney I don't work for the court, I don't work for the judge, I don't work for the government—I work for my client. So if I take your case, from here on in it's me and you, hand in hand, working together on this. You got that?"

"... Yes ma'am."

"OK. Have a seat, Mister Crutchfield. That's what your lawyer should call you when you're in court, 'cause it sounds a whole lot better than 'the defendant.' And you are, in fact, deserving of the term Mister."

She could see he remained wary of her. It worried her, but she pushed on.

"So, are you sure you're good with having me work with you? As your lawyer in your case?"

He glanced at his mother, who nodded and said, "She seem good to me."

"Thanks June, but it's really Jermaine's decision."

June shrugged and fussed with her apron a bit and said, "Jermaine, what do you say?"

"I'm not sure."

Angie nodded. "I understand. Well—let's talk about your case a little. Anything you tell me is confidential. Just between you and me."

He glanced at his mother, who took the hint and left for the kitchen. He waited until she picked up a broom and started sweeping the floor. Then he hitched up his pants and began his tale.

"I have a friend Ronald live over on Ainger Place and a couple weeks ago I was like walking home from there and the jumpouts stopped me and said I matched the 'scription of one the people they said, like, arm-robbed this woman. Said it went down over by Ainger."

"I know Ainger Place. How many people did they say did it?"

"Two."

She remembered being invited into a row house on Ainger with a dirt floor. A lot of crime went down on that street. She wondered what he was doing there and who his friend was.

"I said I didn't do nothin', jus' comin' back from visiting with a friend. But they put handcuffs on me and push me in the car and read me my rights from this card. Say I don't have to talk to them, but I told 'em 'you got the wrong person, I didn't arm rob no one' but they locked me up anyway. Didn't have no gun on me or nothin'."

"Better not have," said June, still in the kitchen.

"I jus' *said*, I didn't have no gun on me."

June told him to watch his mouth and repaired to their tiny bathroom, shaking her head.

Angie gave them a moment and then pressed on. "Remember what you were wearing that night?"

He told her what he was wearing, and she found herself wondering whether the police dispatcher's description of the robbers on the tape of the 911call would match him or the clothing he wore when arrested.

Next she asked him about Ronald: Where did the police find him? Was Ronald's mother home the night of the robbery? Could anyone say what time they left the house on Ainger? She was glad the questions kept coming—she'd worried about forgetting them. She'd learned what drink could do to memory, but hoped she'd caught herself—or been caught by others, like James—in time.

After a while the young man relaxed some. Soon they were sitting on the couch talking. There wasn't much sunlight coming through the window, so Angie figured she should be on her way soon.

"Have you ever been to court before? For any reason?"

"Yeah. They said I stole some beers from the Mini Mart but the charges was dropped. That was the onliest time."

"What about Ronald? Does he have any other charges?"

"He picked up a beef last month."

"What kind of charge?"

". . . I think drugs. Plus they got him on the robbery."

"You ever use drugs?"

" . . . Naw, not really."

June returned to the room. "He's a good boy Miss Donald; he don't do too good in school 'cause he cuts classes, but he's not no criminal."

"Teachers so bad, the more I show the worser I do."

He stared at the floor again and shook his head.

"Jermaine, stop staring at the floor."

Jermaine raised his head just enough to glare at his mother.

"Miss Donald I know it's unbearable hot in here," said June, dabbing her forehead with a washcloth. "You want a glass of ice water? I'm afraid that's all I can offer you."

"Thanks, June, but I was going to . . . well, sure, that would be great."

She waited until June brought her the water and said she'd be in the back and left them alone in the sweltering room again. She talked with Jermaine about the neighborhood, how school was going, and where his father was living these days. He volunteered that Ronald had a gun, but said he didn't have it with him the night of the robbery.

She probed further. As she did, she realized how long it had been since she'd been in the presence of a young black man without means who stood accused of a crime. One on one. Eye to eye with someone who needed her help navigating an unfathomable system.

"Listen, Miss Donna," he said, "I'm gonna tell you the honest truth. Me and Ronald did the robbery. He jus' pulled the gun on the girl as she was walking by. I was surprise as she was. I jus' stood there. He wasn't about shooting her or nothing, I think he jus' wanted money to get some weed and get high. It was stupid. . . . I'm sayin . . . I ain't exac'ly rollin in the hot sauce, but I got a hundred dollars saved up and if you could fix me up so's I could get a pay lawyer to take my case I'd appreciate it."

"Jermaine I was a pay lawyer. I've been paid thousands of dollars to try cases. Murders, drug deals, you name it. I'm taking your case for free because a friend at PDS said you would need a new lawyer, and the judge who has your case said he'd appoint me if—"

"Oh. I didn't know you was a pay lawyer. Why—"

"Let's just focus on what happened. Did you say anything when he took the gun out?"

"Jus' said, 'What the fuck you doing?' And he told me to shut up."

She nodded and almost smiled at his response, knowing if it went down that way, he wasn't culpable: he had a mere presence defense. In which case, the charge should be tried to a jury. But it was too early to tell—he could have helped; they could have split the money afterward. He could be lying.

As he filled her in on the details, she realized she *knew* this kid, knew more about his situation than he did himself—and yes, she wanted to help him. This kid who was surely not rollin' in the hot sauce, and might never be.

Her eyes were drawn back to the Woolworth's window shades. All of a sudden she felt she'd been in this very room before. That wasn't the case, yet the room felt familiar. As if she'd been there in a dream, or earlier in her life, or in another life. All the same it felt right to be there.

Of course she'd had feelings like this before, back when she was really drunk, ready to pass out and the rooms went spinning. That feeling of "been here before," just before the blackout. But this was a different sort of déjà vu.

He asked if she'd mind if he stepped outside with her for a moment, while he had a cigarette. She said all right and he unlocked the bolt and opened the door for her and they walked outside and stood on the porch. The sun had dipped below the skyline in the west and clouds were gathering, but heat continued to bake the blacktop. The effect was like walking past the open door of a furnace. The air so thick and close she thought it would explode when he struck a match to light a cigarette. A Kool, she noticed. The brand she used to smoke.

"It's godawful hot but my mom won't let me smoke in the house. Plus I got a question about something I don't want her to hear."

"All right," she said. *God am I thirsty*, she thought. *But only for water.*

He took a slow drag on the Kool before proceeding.

"I'm wonderin' how much time would I have to do if I was found guilty?"

"After a trial?"

"Yeah, I guess."

The question gave her pause and she thought about it, knowing her answer would disappoint him. She told him a few years, possibly five for a first offense, but that at this point she couldn't really say. He looked away from her after she delivered that rock hard truth. While he did, she stared at him and digested the thought: He had a lot at stake. It wasn't about her and her drinking problem. It was whether she'd be able to represent him well. It was about the rest of his life.

"Man, I'd be twenty-three, time I get out. I ain't got that kinda time to burn . . . I got things I want to do."

She turned to look at him again. He stood there smoking, staring in the general direction of the street, shaking his head. Then he took another puff on his Kool and flicked its burning stub into the dusk.

She thought of Ken Mundy. He was a great trial lawyer from days past, when she was just starting out. He would get this kid off in a heartbeat. Could she? He didn't need a lawyer who was rusty and jumpy.

"You hangin' with any of the neighborhood crews?"

"Naw. I mostly jus' try to stay out their way." He bit down on his lower lip, just as his mother had done.

"Jermaine, I'll take your case if you're comfortable having me as your lawyer. And I'll do everything I can for you."

He looked her in the eyes for a second before answering.

"Yeah, that be cool. You seem like you good, and you come all the way out here too . . . so we good, we good."

"OK now. Listen up: I don't want you to talk to anyone

about this case except me. Not Ronald, not the police, not even your mother. But I need you to tell me exactly what happened, in order to do right by you. Understand?"

"I do, yeah."

They went back inside and sat on the couch again. She took a pen and yellow pad out of her bag.

"Let's go through what happened once more. Why don't you start by telling me what you remember about the girl?"

"Ok but first I got to use the bathroom."

She nodded and he stood and turned and walked away. She figured it was a good thing he did because she was now filled to the brim with emotion.

She watched him walk toward the back of the house. Too long a pause on the drug question. At least he was scared, that was a good sign. He may have committed a crime—that wasn't clear yet; she'd have to hunt down the facts. He was angry, but who wasn't? There was still something untamed in him, something inside that didn't want to accept the bad hand he'd been dealt. Defendants like that had always been her favorites.

His gait was that of a child—make that manchild—with a bit of a strut. Who miracle of miracles, was only just beginning to be infected by the street. She'd represented kids like him in the early days, back in Juvie. She watched him until he disappeared behind the curtain they'd strung across the back of the living room to create something close to a separate bedroom.

A former client's image welled up from somewhere inside her, and then another one, and she understood why: this kid was them once, just starting down the path. But not this time, she vowed, not this one.

June returned to the dayroom, looking even more drawn and worried.

"It's going to be all right, Mrs. Crutchfield."

"I hope so. He's a good boy, I promise."

Angie nodded. "I know." *They all say that*, she told herself.

"June," she said. "I cut my teeth on cases like this, so I know what he's going through. I'll do my best for him."

It was another half hour before she left the house, armed with all the facts Jermaine could tell her about the case. She walked to her car, thinking James had probably been home for hours and was wondering where she was.

A storm had come and gone and the evening sky had cleared. The courthouse was closed by now and the day's funerals were over. She stood by the Jetta for a moment, keys in hand, and took in the scene. She was about a mile and a half south of the Capitol building. The light was shining in its chiseled white cupola. The statue of a young woman—Columbia—stood atop it, her gaze fixed on the eastern horizon, as if—

Her thoughts were interrupted by the buzz of her cell phone. It was Kadisha, wondering if she'd met with Jermaine yet.

"I did, I'm leaving his house now. He's a good kid and I'm psyched! He may have a mere presence defense, it could go—possibly, could go to trial based on what he told me! Of course I'll have to check it all out, but—I met his mom, spent time with them and I want so much to help this kid out, he has no record and—"

"That's great, Angie, and I know you're excited to be back, but try not to get so carried away; you sound—"

"I sound what?"

"Sweetie you've known this kid for an hour and already I can hear it in your voice."

"Hear what? I'm only—"

"I know you and I'm saying, I can hear it in your voice. One hour and you're ready to risk your life in back alleys to find witnesses, pull all-nighters to be brilliant in closing, do whatever in hell it takes for him—"

"I'll do what it takes to represent him right, that's all. And I like this kid, so—"

"Please, represent him well and that will be enough. I'm saying, already you sound like you're on a mission: get him off or else."

"Sure, well, that's what motivates me *all the time*, watching them walk out of the courtroom *free men*, heading back to the block with their heads held high once the contest is over. I mean, the wanting to win part, the dream of slaying the dragon, is—you know, snatching a defendant in distress from that soul-crushing process that —so often— leads to the Big House is—"

"Angie, listen to yourself. Can you just, just take it one step at a time?"

"Sorry K, it's how I'm built; it's always a battle to keep these kids out of these places we know are nothing but, nothing but wretched, overcrowded—"

"I know—"

"So yeah, I want to win for them, get them that second chance, and then . . . K, are you there?"

". . . Uh-huh. I'm here. Listening to you bust a gut over how bad you want to set everyone free. But I have to tell you yet again: Calm. It. Down. You sound so supercharged you're making me afraid. For you, not for him."

"Sorry. I'm just excited, I'm not about to head for some

bar now and drink myself under the floor over this. I mean it."

"OK, good. One step at a time. What do they say at AA?"

"They say stick with people who are supportive. So stop all this worry, be supportive, and I'll be fine!"

". . . Well. All right. Call me tomorrow and we'll finish the paperwork with Judge Stern."

After Kadisha hung up, Angie took a last look at the statue of Columbia and chirped the Jetta. She started to get into the car, then paused and took a deep breath. She tried pushing the thought away but it pushed right back.

She didn't want to, but now she understood. Yes, it was the white-hot intensity of the feelings she'd just expressed that had made her so successful . . . but that intensity was not all good. Sometimes it felt like a fire raging inside her, one that could be contained and sated and extinguished only by something even stronger, something that could manage it, douse it, something like . . . drink. Only drink had taken the edge off, only drink had kept her unconscious at night, only drink had made it possible for her to get enough sleep to recharge for the morrow.

The thought rattled her, but she had to thank AA for it, as well as Kadisha. Step Four of AA's Twelve Step program required her to conduct a "searching and fearless" examination of her past and present behavior. An honest assessment of her strengths and weaknesses. So K was right; she needed think it through. Figure out what exactly she was doing to herself in taking this case.

She'd often said she'd "go to the wall" for her clients. And she always did, because . . . she couldn't help herself. Yeah baby, the need to win for them: it was the Kool-Aid she couldn't stay away from. The primary addiction, the one that led to the other one.

For a second she remembered riding in her silver Mercedes, before the crash—weaving down the road laughing as its speakers boomed out Happy Hour rock and roll. That jazzy feeling! But it was memory only, the mad blur of the past, and she needed to keep it that way. K was right, she needed to moderate her passion, do what she could for her client, that and no more, and stifle the urge to wage war on his behalf. If she could do that, she would be all right. But could she? She took a deep breath and uttered a vow of moderation in all things.

But after that she took a last look at the statue of the young woman in the cupola. The woman was eternally on guard, ready to sound the alarm, determined to fight the good fight on behalf of her people. It was impressive, it was... inspiring.

She slid into the Jetta and fired up its engine. It was getting late. It was time to head home, have a quick dinner with James and go over her notes. In the morning, she'd give Judge Stern a call, then get started: she needed to line up an investigator, she had to run records checks, she had to get discovery. She had to draft and file motions and subpoena the radio run, that too, and then investigate the case, find—

She took a deep, calming breath. She'd be OK. She just had to prepare for court. In moderation, though—to be sure.

Death By Grand Jury

Tyrone Jeffries paused before entering the sunbaked brick building, looked to see if trouble lurked to his left or right, and drew a long stream of unfiltered tobacco into his lungs. He savored the mix for a while, then blew it out again, puckering his lips like a fish to produce smoke rings.

Observing this, Detective King glared at him, swore, and began stabbing a finger repeatedly in the direction of the building's front door. Jeffries had to smile at that — when making an arrest in the projects, his usual approach was to storm the barricades, crash through the doorway brandishing his weapon, and roust the bad guys out before they quite knew "whazzup." In those situations, Alex King always lagged behind, hampered by what Jeffries viewed as a paralyzing blend of fear and insecurity.

But this morning, all they had to do was serve a subpoena on a witness and take her for a ride downtown, so King was Tarzan with a badge on, ready to lead the charge. Jeffries considered responding to King with his raised middle finger, but checked the impulse. It was way too hot for a fistfight, and besides they had work to do.

King dismissed Jeffries with a wave of the hand and took off for the building, clutching his hip holster, as if the dwelling were full to the brim with felons. Jeffries, having been there before, knew it wasn't. Of course it wasn't felon-free either, but it was eight a.m., and in his experience felons were not early risers. He smiled as he watched King advance, knowing he'd falter before entering, stop before the door and wait for backup.

Benning Terrace seemed sound asleep and at peace with the world this oppressive August morning. The dark clouds moving in signaled rain, but Jeffries figured the stale Anacostia air was so humid the storm would not last long, much less cool things down south of the river. The drops would just hit the sidewalk, sizzle and become steam. It was a typical D.C. summer.

It was also quiet, perhaps too quiet. They had parked the unmarked a little too far away to run for it if things went third rail, but Jeffries didn't care one way or the other. Why postpone the inevitable? He remembered his shrink telling him he may as well wear a sign saying "kill me" when he went out alone to break into killers' dens, throttle them, and bring them downtown. "Kill me sign, great idea," he'd told her. "I'll paint the words in red." She'd responded by telling him she understood how painful it must be to lose a daughter but it was close to three years now and getting himself killed wouldn't bring Alicia back. They hadn't finished that particular session—he'd blown up and stormed out.

He flicked his cigarette and sauntered up the sidewalk, opening his arms wide to make his chest a perfect target for those so inclined, but nothing happened. King stood waiting at the door for him. Jeffries brushed by him and shoved the heavy metal door open with his shoulder.

"I was just about to go in," King complained.

"Thought you were waiting for a bus, you were standing here so long," said Jeffries.

The open door revealed an empty, unadorned cinder-block foyer. Jeffries' gaze took in a row of silver mailboxes built into the wall to his right, matching apartment doors on each side of the foyer past the mailboxes, and a cement staircase leading to the second and third floors. Inside, everything was neat, clean and shiny; the painted walls—two tones of green—were graffiti-free. The stair steps, covered with stainless-steel tread, led directly to an open, entirely visible second-floor landing built that way so no one could lie in wait there. Beyond that there would be a ninety-degree turn revealing another flight of stairs, which would lead upward, over their heads, toward the front of the building. There it would open on a second-floor foyer exactly like the first.

Jeffries held up his hand like a soldier sensing the enemy. They stood still and listened. Silence, except for the sound of hip-hop music coming from behind one of the apartment doors.

"A little background music would help," he said, taking stock of the metal and cement décor, the bland green walls, the coldness of the clean, open lines. He knew the look. He'd been in enough projects to realize Benning Terrace was built the same way they built prisons, probably by the same construction company. Sure, the place was filled with apartments, not cells, but the overall effect was the same: twentieth-century prison design posing as a low-income city dwelling. No wonder so many of his brothers and sisters wound up in the Big House sooner or later. No place like home.

The music, which came from behind the door to apartment 103, hipped and hopped on. Jeffries signaled "let's go" and they took the stairs two at a time, making the second floor in half a minute. Apartment 201 was to their left. Jeffries knocked sharply on the door and took a subpoena from his pants pocket.

"Who is it?" asked a wary female voice from within.

"D.C. Police," King replied. They waited, listening to the rumble and screech of metal, followed by fumbling with a latch; the door was both locked and barred from the inside.

"Security Saves Lives," King whispered to Jeffries in the interim. Jeffries just glared at him.

Finally the door opened a few inches, revealing a fortyish woman with a worried look on her face. Jeffries had seen this look before. She asked him what he wanted.

"Ms. Brown?" The woman nodded. "We need to talk to your daughter Kimberly about a certain matter."

"Can you tell me what you want her for? She hasn't done nothin' wrong." Then, in a lower voice, "And she don't know nothin' about what happened last spring, neither."

"We need to ask her a few questions about that very thing, ma'am," King added.

Ms. Brown's eyes scanned the foyer. She seemed relieved to see that the other doors on her floor remained closed. Jeffries thrust a piece of paper through the opening of the door. As she took hold of it, he told her the blunt truth: "Subpoena. We gotta take Kimberly downtown for about an hour, no big deal."

As Ms. Brown unfolded the subpoena, a sleepy-eyed teenaged girl with her hair in cornrows appeared next to her.

"What's going on?" she asked, and watching the woman glare at the girl, Jeffries knew it was Kimberly even before her mother tried to slam the door shut on them. He stomped his foot on the floor just past the threshold, braced his leg against the metal door and shoved it open. The women stepped back, the detectives moved forward, and by the time Brown said, "Kimmy, run!" Jeffries and King were inside the apartment.

Before the girl could figure out which way to go, Jeffries grabbed her by the arm and bellowed "Gotcha in my death grip; move and you die!" She opted not to move.

"Look," he said, spinning her around and squaring her up before him. "No one is going to hurt you. Don't make this any harder than it has to be." Something inside him cringed when he said things like this; made him feel like a cardboard cop in a movie with a bad script. Maybe he'd heard another cop use lines like this years back, and over time the words had congealed in his long-term memory, waiting to be uttered in tight moments when he went on automatic pilot. Or maybe it was much simpler: he'd become the cop in the bad movie by now, and the bad movie was his life.

"The quicker we get out of here, the less likely anyone's going to notice," offered King. This too was a line they'd used many times, but it was important to say when snatching a witness because it seemed that when neighbors noticed what was going down, they told the wrong people, and witnesses like Kimberly were less likely to survive their homecoming.

"Where you takin' her?" Ms. Brown asked.

"Downtown, the U.S. Attorney's office," offered King.

"Grand jury," added Jeffries, and mother and daughter froze. Then Ms. Brown looked at the subpoena more closely and let out a sharp cry, like she'd been pricked by a pin.

"Oh no, you're not takin' my baby down the gran' jury, no!" she declared, grabbing hold of the girl's arm.

It was just enough resistance to jump-start the detectives again. Jeffries reeled the girl back in while King grappled with her mother. Seconds later Jeffries slapped a double arm bar on the squirming teen, and they bulled their way back out the door like linebackers fighting for crucial yardage.

Somehow Ms. Brown managed to shake loose from King. She threw herself on Jeffries' back and snaked an arm around his neck in an effort to make him to let go of her daughter. That was it for King; in one fury-filled motion he ripped her off Jeffries' back and threw her to the floor. He had his Glock out and pointed at her before she could get up.

"I don't shoot to wound," he seethed, "so stand up slowly."

She complied right away, raising her hands above her head even before he told her to do so.

While King guarded Ms. Brown, Jeffries yelled "Airborne," lifted Kimberly off her feet and held her aloft as he made his way down the stairs, out the door, and toward the Impala. She kicked her feet the entire time, mostly fanning the air, but every so often landing a sneakered heel squarely on his thigh. As he neared the unmarked, he hoisted her on his left hip and held her around the waist with one hand. She wailed and scratched at the air. He drew his keys from his pocket with his free hand, chirped the rear door of the cruiser open, and was about to toss her into the back seat like a ragdoll when he stopped himself. He took a breath, plunked the girl down firmly but carefully, and slammed the car door shut.

He turned to see King marching Kimberly's mother down the walkway toward him. He walked about ten feet behind her, gun still drawn.

"Think we can do without the gun, Alex. Put it away."

"I said she could come downtown with us if she behaved herself," King said.

"That's just great, Alex," observed Jeffries. "Why not make this as hard as it can be?" He'd been through all this many times and knew exactly how it would play out if they took the girl's mother with them. Indeed he had anticipated mother and daughter fireworks the second he and King were dispatched to pick the girl up from the Terrace and bring her downtown to testify. But he hadn't expected Ms. Brown to struggle so ferociously, to cling so tenaciously to her daughter as he dragged her away, to do everything but claw her way into the cruiser with one purpose in mind: to snatch her girl from the jaws of the U.S. Attorney's Office and the fate that often followed witnesses who testified before grand juries in drug-related murder cases: death by handgun or shotgun. Usually, death inflicted by a shot to the temple while the victim was on her knees begging to be spared.

Knowing this, what remained of the better part of Jeffries' nature respected Ms. Brown's over-the-top effort to safeguard her daughter. The former Ms. Jeffries would probably have done the same thing if the situation had presented itself, not that their daughter was ever an innocent teen like Kimberly. No, their daughter—his daughter—had track marks on her arms, the death virus in her blood, and a vacant look in her eyes the last time he'd seen her. By the time she was Kimberly's age, she'd probably had sex more often than he'd had, with more men than he could count. But at least she was alive then.

"Are you arresting us?" asked Ms. Brown carefully.

"Not just yet," barked Jeffries, "but get physical with me again, I'm gonna slap a felony on you. Assault on a police officer, five years, you don't get to pick the prison."

"Easy, 'Dog" cautioned King, "she's OK now."

"Yeah well I been in this movie too many times," Jeffries replied. "Too many times. But somehow I never get used to being shoved, kicked, and bit. And since both you ladies are so good at that, I'm gonna cuff you while I lick my wounds.

Let's hop to it, Alex. I don't want nobody grabbin' me by the throat while I'm driving across the Anacostia Bridge."

King grunted his agreement and they cuffed the women, who sat in sullen silence as the detectives slammed the doors, fired up the Impala and gunned it down the street.

"All in a day's work," muttered King. "Man, it's good to be dodging potholes instead of bullets."

"Two years and a wake-up," said Jeffries. "If I make it that long. Then I'm done this motherfucker."

II

Ms. Brown had barely begun speaking when the prosecutor cut her off.

"Hold on a minute, Ms. Brown," he said, "while I look over the case file. By the way, I'm Assistant United States Attorney Scott Collins, and I'm handling the case your daughter's involved in."

Jeffries, who was standing in the doorway to Collins' office, sighed and shook his head. "Seen this flick too," he muttered.

"What's that?" asked Collins.

"I said, 'See what you can do.'"

"You sure?"

"Sure I'm sure. Don't stop on my account."

"Rook thought you were gonna give him some advice," King whispered.

Jeffries simply stared at King, instead of saying what he wanted to say.

"Ms. Brown," began Collins, "you see—"

"You don't seem to understand," interrupted Ms. Brown. "My daughter don't know a thing about no murder. She's sixteen and in the eleventh grade. She don't know none a them street hoodlums."

"But see the police report says—"

"Can you please put those papers down a minute and at least *look* at me when I'm talkin'? Jesus God."

"Ssshh, Mom be quiet," said the sixteen-year-old, placing her hands on her slim tween hips. Jeffries recognized the defiant stance immediately.

"Don't tell me to be quiet, don't tell me that!" Ms. Brown said, sticking her face within a short hot breath of her daughter's mouth. "And stand up straight and get your hands off your hips!"

Kimberly gave her mother a sharp look, but Ms. Brown didn't flinch, and after a few seconds the girl broke eye contact and looked away.

"Now tell the man, Kimba," urged Ms. Brown.

". . . OK. But she's right. I don't know nothing about Fruit Loops getting shot."

"Let's call him by his proper name," said Collins. "Ricardo, right?"

Another mistake, thought Jeffries. *Dear God in heaven, spare me from rookies.*

"Yeah, Ricardo, that's his name but no one calls him that. I mean, called him that when . . . ."

"Poor child," said Ms. Brown.

"Anyway like I tole you, I was on the playground that night with my friends, but I left before nine o'clock."

"Now, you weren't wearing a watch that night, were you," suggested Collins.

Jeffries cringed: Another counterproductive correction. As if to confirm Jeffries' thought, the girl clammed and glanced at her mother.

"She's not never allowed to stay in the street past nine," offered Ms. Brown. "Never."

Collins picked a loose thread off the lapel of his grey glen plaid suit, closed the file and placed it gently on the desktop. Jeffries knew he was stalling for time, trying to figure out where to take the questioning next. Despite his professional dress and demeanor, the young man's smooth-skinned face and full crop of dark hair made Jeffries think of him as a schoolboy. A youngster, still learning his trade. There was also something familiar about him, something that made Jeffries dislike him even more than he disliked most new Assistant U.S. Attorneys. He felt like he'd seen him before, but couldn't remember where. He also suspected the young man had no sense of the street-level consequences of what he was doing.

Collins glanced briefly at Jeffries, who gave him the green light in the form of a knowing wink. It was totally fake, but the prosecutor took it as encouragement. He nodded, swallowed, and began again.

"See Kimberly, we have a witness in the neighborhood who says you saw 'Slim Jim' Carter march young Ric—OK, young Fruit Loops—down the block to his Mercedes about half an hour before they found him."

Collins looked up at Jeffries again, saw he was nodding approval, and edged closer to girl. He spoke quietly, trying to make it seem like he and the child were friends sharing a relaxed, intimate moment. Jeffries began to think the rook had a few brain cells after all; maybe they had a chance. After all, they wouldn't be able to indict Carter without the girl's testimony.

"We know Slim Jim killed Fruit Loops," Collins continued, "and your testimony is important because it shows he made the boy get in his car, three blocks from the dumpster, shortly before he was killed. Kimberly: All you have to do is testify you saw that happen."

"Just tell them what you told Detective Jeffries on our ride downtown: what you saw while you were on that playground with your buds that night," said King.

"Remember, nobody is asking you to say Slim was the killer, or that you saw the shooting go down," added the prosecutor, giving the girl a one-shoulder shrug to signal it was no big deal.

Nice move, Jeffries had to acknowledge, he'd used the one-shoulder shrug himself when working a witness.

Collins glanced at his watch. "Like Detective King said, you already told Detective Jeffries Slim was there and that Loops got into his car around nine that night. See Kimberly, what you saw is just a tiny piece of the puzzle. Just some information about what you observed. You could be in and out of the grand jury room in ten minutes," the young man said, pointing to the hallway just beyond Jeffries. "Shall we go?"

Kimberly shifted her weight from one foot to the other, adjusted a pink braid in her hair, frowned, and looked toward her mother once more for support. Ms. Brown stood up, folded her arms and shook her head.

"I am not goin' to let you make my daughter testify in there," she said. "I'll sue you if I have to."

"You can't sue us, Ms. Brown," said Collins. "We're the government. Besides, we're on your side in all this. We're trying to help." He stood up, cleared his throat and said, "Detective Jeffries?"

As Jeffries moved toward the girl, Ms. Brown fell to her knees, clasped her hands together as if to pray and began sobbing, "No, no, no, don't take my baby; don't make her do this, please!"

Both King and Collins looked away, daunted by the sheer emotional force of the plea. Jeffries just stared at the woman, feeling very little and telling himself not to care.

Kimberly began to tear up, then grabbed her mother by the arm and cried "It's OK, Mamma, I won't do it; I'm not testifying 'fore no grand jury!"

King, muttering "fucking chaos around here," shut the door to the hallway to muffle the sound. Collins stood still, rubbing his chin as if there were stubble on it, then cleared his throat again and adjusted his tie. He looked over at Jeffries, who grunted his disgust and turned away. He turned next to King, but King offered no help either. "Let it blow over," King said, keeping his eyes on the grey government-issue carpet that covered the floor. A moment later he left the room.

Soon the gale force of the mother and daughter's plea resolved itself into small gusts of shuddering and sobbing. They held onto one another in a tight embrace, even as their emotions receded. The moment wound down until silence ruled the room. Jeffries nodded and headed for the door as the prosecutor began telling Kimba about her legal obligation to testify, and how he was going to make her honor it. "That's my job, and I'll do it to protect both you and your community," he intoned.

Jeffries sighed. It was "the speech." He left for the grand jury room.

"With your cooperation, we can lock Slim Jim up for good," Jeffries said with exaggerated earnestness, quoting from the speech as he walked down the hallway. He knew the words by heart and was glad to be out of the room so he didn't have to hear the rest of them. All the prosecutors used it. He wondered if it was printed on some handout they made them memorize at D.A. school, or when they were new to the office and stumbling through misdemeanors.

As he was about to enter the grand jury room to make sure they were ready for Kimberly, he realized some small part of him that had not yet become numb in the line of duty was rooting for the girl and her mother. He dismissed the thought immediately—*this is nothing out of the ordinary*, he told himself. *We haul kids like Kimberly downtown eight days a week—it's just part of the process of indicting some piece of street slime who's offed a neighbor.*

"Tough luck," he told the Assistant U.S. Attorney handling the grand jury. "Girl was in the wrong place at the right time, and that makes her a key fact witness for the government. Simple as that. We got to lock in her testimony before Slim's posse gets to her, one way or another. That's all."

Still, anger and adrenalin surged in his chest and he found himself hoping he'd be the one to arrest James "Slim Jim" Carter, a seasoned hit man if there ever was one. Maybe there'd be a shootout. Maybe Carter would die before trial, and the Browns would live happily ever after. "And maybe I'm the King of Siam," he added, putting a cap on that line of thought.

The grand jury attorney said they were ready to hear the girl's testimony, so Jeffries did an about-face and made his way back to the witness room, entering just as Collins was reaching the climax of his spiel.

"So we'll spare no effort to protect you," the young man was saying, "and I will personally see to it that you are placed in our, ah, very successful witness protection program until the defendant has been tried and sentenced."

"Yeah, good luck on that front," Jeffries found himself saying. Collins gave him a sharp look, to which Jeffries replied, "You know the stats, kid."

The rook's face immediately began turning red, but Kimberly and her mother didn't react. They sat silently, spent and resigned, heads bowed and eyes to the floor. As if awaiting sentence for a crime they themselves had committed. At that moment, Jeffries remembered who the prosecutor reminded him of: the young, cocksure intern he and his former wife had met in the emergency room when they brought Alicia there after she'd injured her ankle playing basketball. The intern had told them it was a sprain, but a few painful practices later they realized he'd been wrong. It was a fracture. He'd thought of the intern as a student too. Alicia had been a good basketball player, he told himself for the ten-thousandth time, too bad she... yeah, too bad. It was all too bad, why think about it.

Just then King breezed into the room all smiles, like he was arriving at a party.

"Hey, OK Kimberly, time to go," he said. "Nonchalance is everything," he added *sotto voce* for the benefit of Jeffries and the rook. As King took hold of the girl by the shoulder and forearm, Jeffries reminded himself to get busy finding a new partner.

"Gently," said Collins, eyeballing King as Jeffries moved deftly between Kimberly and her mother.

Ms. Brown and her daughter looked at one another for a moment, then the girl dropped her eyes and said, "Fine, let's go" and King led her from the room. Careful not to look at Ms. Brown, King shut the door behind them.

After they left, Jeffries heard King assuring the girl they were all on the same side, that they would do everything in their power to keep her safe, etc. and etc. "The less likely something is to be true, the more we repeat it," he said under his breath.

"Look. What the heck's the matter with you," said Collins.

"Girl may as well wear a bulls-eye on her chest from now on."

"We've doing everything we can do to protect her."

"That's what I'm afraid of."

"Detective—"

"Don't let me keep you from calling witness protection."

"I'll take care of that. Don't tell me how to do my job."

"It's not a matter of how—it's a matter of when. Make the call."

"Detective, if I need to get you off this case, I'm prepared to do it. Don't push me."

Jeffries had an answer for that, but managed not to say it. He clamped his mouth shut and kept it shut as the rook smoothed his silk tie, gathered his files and left the room.

III

He was supposed to see the shrink after his shift, but decided not to. He wasn't in the mood for talk. It wasn't all that complicated anyway. In addition to the depression caused by the death of his daughter, he'd been told he had post-traumatic stress syndrome. It was the natural result of seeing too many bodies on the ground. Dead ones, dying ones, limp ones, stiff ones. Bodies found in alleyways, bedrooms, and street corners, soaking in puddles of blood. People shot dead and shot again for emphasis. And always, somewhere on the scene, near the scene, or lurking in the background as motive, drugs.

Shortly after Alicia died, he had given up on the painstaking detective work needed to identify and nab killers. The '90s were a bitch, and life was too short. Why spend months hunting down evidence, he'd decided, when you knew they'd beat the charge one way or another: kill a witness, hire a bleeding-heart defense attorney to bamboozle the jurors, make a deal, turn in some big-shots, do whatever it took. No matter how they got off, sooner or later they'd get back in the game and kill again. So he'd made an adjustment. Changed his approach. Whenever a killer left clues to his identity at the scene, Jeffries made the case by himself, tracking the tough guy down and arresting him wherever he found him: in his bed, in his Benz, on the block, wherever.

A few months later, he'd stormed into a crack house in a rage, all by himself, gun drawn. Grabbed the punk killer he'd come for, threw him down the stairs, scraped him off the floor, cuffed him, and dragged him by one leg to the cruiser—all before the gunmen in the house caught their breath and even thought about drawing their heat. That was the pinch that earned him the nickname "Bad Dog," but there were others even more reckless. Some homicide detectives thought he was crazy, a wild man, but others worshipped him for bulldozing into the world's worst situations without a care. Dodging bullets, kicking away knives, snarling and cursing and putting the grab on the bad boys all by himself. The stuff of legend, as long as he lived.

At first he thought it had to do with being a veteran detective. Seeing it all and still standing, until eventually fear—both the idea and the sensation of it—drifted out of his consciousness, like smoke dissolving in the wind. Simple enough to suss: experience makes you fearless. But as the months wore on and he continued to raise the stakes on himself, suffering the occasional flesh wound, enduring the occasional beating, he began to realize he had no fear because he had no great desire to live.

To put it another way, with his wife gone and his daughter dead, he didn't mind dying because he had nothing to live for. People died every day, so what? Why not him too? The shrink called that the thinking of a depressed person and wanted to talk about it for weeks, but he'd finally connected the dots, sat her down and told her how it was in the real world outside her paneled office with the framed paintings of people dancing: it would be easy to think he'd been so dedicated to the job he'd lost his family along the way, but that wasn't quite the case. He'd only done what the job demanded, which was long hours, no letup and shifts that changed each time his body got used to one. It took a few sessions for the shrink to understand what he meant when he told her "shift work destroyed my family."

"Perhaps there were other factors as well. Do you think your own behavior had anything to do with it?" she had asked.

He explained: "When you work midnights, you get home at sunrise and no one's there. Kid's in school, wife's at work. You down a few beers. You sleep, you get up, you spend your spare time alone. By the time they come home you're getting ready to go. It's hi and bye. If you work four-to-midnights, it's worse: they're gone before you get up, and you get back after they're asleep. Most contact occurs when you make too much noise getting ready for bed and wake your sleeping wife up. You figure the day shift will work out since the whole family's doing nine to five, but most of the time day shifts end in the night 'cause someone died in the afternoon, and when you do get home it's dark and all you are to them is the guy who's never there."

"They get used to your not being around. For a while they're even proud of it. You're out there solving murders, protecting the community; they miss you. But sooner or later, they get tired of your showing up late, or not at all, for family events. School meetings, basketball, anniversaries, holiday dinners, track meets—the death squads don't take time off, so neither do you. A few years of this, one day your woman wakes up, realizes she's seen you about two hours that week, that it's been that way for months, and decides she needs a new life. While you go through all that, your kid withdraws, starts spending nights with friends you never get to meet. Finds a new family, Mr. and Mrs. Opiate and their many close relatives, and by the time you catch up with her she's not into track no more, she's into track marks."

"That . . . makes a lot of sense," the shrink had said.

"Cool. That'll be three hundred bucks, and if you stick around I'll write you a prescription," he'd replied, leaving her speechless before leaving her office.

IV

The sun was in the west, an orange ball making for the horizon, as the Browns left the four-story, glass-enclosed U.S. Attorney's office.

"I didn't see anyone from the neighborhood the whole time we was there," Ms. Brown said. "We're doin' good." Then she noticed a line of cars parked on the south side of the well-kept square they were crossing. Fancy, late-model cars gleaming in the post-storm sunlight. Young men stood leaning against them, at twenty or thirty-foot intervals, looking through binoculars trained on the square. Or more likely the people in it, she realized, and her heart sank faster than a brick in water.

"What is it, Mamma?" asked Kimberly, squinting and shielding her eyes from the sunlight.

"Nothing," was Doretta Brown's barely audible reply. But the next moment she made a hard turn toward the northern edge of the square, grabbed Kimberly by the hand and whispered "Follow me" with such intensity that her daughter obeyed without objection for the first time in weeks. She saw a bus round the corner and approach the street bordering the northern side of the square. "That looks like the K5; shake a tail feather and we'll catch it on the corner. Come on now," she urged, and they took off for the bus, running as if Slim Jim himself followed hard upon them.

Jeffries watched from his Mercury as they ran, yelling and waving their arms like drowning swimmers. The bus picked up speed and roared past them, leaving a dark monoxide cloud in its wake. It would always turn out like this for them, he thought. He tried not to think it but knew as well as he knew his own name that even if death in the form of Slim Jim Carter didn't find them, life would pass them by much like the bus driver did. He watched as Ms. Brown stopped on the sidewalk near the cross street to catch her breath. He fought the impulse to help them, even as he watched her heaving and panting. But it didn't take all that long before he decided that since he'd dragged them downtown, he owed them a ride home.

He pulled his dark blue Mercury Capri up to the curb beside the Browns, got their attention with a short, sharp double honk, lowered the passenger-side window and told them to get in, pushing the door open with his long arm.

"Why should we?" asked Ms. Brown after she collected herself. "Las' time you played it pretty damn rough with the both of us."

"Self defense," he replied. "I had no choice. A subpoena's a court order, you know. Plus you damn near choked me to death."

They hesitated. Ms. Brown looked over her shoulder to see if the young bloods from the cars were coming her way.

"They can't see you now, the building's blocking the view. Look, I'm trying to help you out here."

"You mean you'll give us a ride home?"

"If that's what you want. Main thing is to get you somewhere safe."

"What you think, Kimmy?"

Kimberly took some time to make up her mind. She looked around to see if anyone was approaching. Then she looked down and drew a few imaginary lines on the sidewalk with her sneaker before responding.

". . . May as well get in, Mamma. Can't win for losin' today."

"Jump in the back seat and stay down low," Jeffries ordered, and within seconds they were in the car, riding west toward K Street, Union Station and the bus terminals. No one spoke. In the silence they all watched a sleek silver train make its way down the Red Line rails, bathed in the pale late afternoon sunlight.

"Why we goin' home?" asked the girl. "That's dumb. They'll jus' ride over an' shoot us there," she said flatly.

"You got a point, child," Jeffries said. "Time they get street police over there to protect you, there'll be nothin' left to protect. May as well call it a witness prevention program."

"Why's that?" asked the mother.

"Never mind."

"I know why," said the girl. "It *prevents* witnesses from testifyin' at trial, cause by then they're dead."

"That's just great."

"You know, Miss Brown, your girl's got a lot of potential," Jeffries said as he eased the car onto a vacant construction site just off New York Avenue. He killed the engine and turned sideways so he could address them directly.

"You all got relatives out of town you can go to?"

"No," said the girl.

"Then I don't know if I can help you."

There was a pause. Ms. Brown looked out the window for inspiration.

"Ah—in Richmond we do," she offered.

"Richmond," he repeated, without inflection. "I know Richmond. Tell me more."

"My brother-in-law lives there."

"What's his name?"

"Well see we're not the best of friends since my husband left out on us an' all. Blamin' everything—"

"What's his name and address?" asked Jeffries. Kimberly shot her mother a what-are-you-crazy look while he took a pen and note pad out of his glove compartment.

Ms. Brown didn't say anything.

"OK, I'll try again. What's the brother-in-law's name," he asked.

"Ah—Loftus. James Loftus."

"That's a start. This James Loftus got an address?"

"I can't remember the street right now, but . . . ."

"Uh-huh. Well I was gonna drop you off the bus station, give you enough cash to get somewheres safe with someone you know, but . . . don't lie to me now, can you stay at your brother-in-law's place or not? Assuming you can figure out where it is in Richmond."

"Oh sure, he'll put us up. Won't like it but you know, he'll do it," Brown said, suddenly sounding quite confident.

"OK then," Jeffries said, offering her his cell phone. "How 'bout you give him a call then and make sure he's willing to put you up."

"Ah—I don't have his number, but I sure do know where he stay at. He'll let us stay with him."

"You sure about that now?"

"Uh-huh."

As Jeffries stuffed his cell back in his pocket, Kimberly wrinkled her brow and turned her head slightly toward her mother. She had a scrunched up, perplexed look on her face, as if she didn't understand why on earth the woman was saying these things. Jeffries saw enough of her expression in his rear view to confirm what he already suspected.

"Cause I'd hate to see you get down there an' have no place to go but some shelter," he added.

Neither of the women said anything in reply. Another silver train made its way down the Red Line track while Jeffries considered the options.

"What do you do for money?" he asked.

"Cleaning lady. I temp in the office buildings downtown, and all."

"You party?"

"*No*, I don't party. I work and I clean and—and make sure she got decent clothes to wear to school and does her homework."

He didn't have an answer for that, but was glad to hear it. She'd said it in a way that left no room for doubt.

"Let's drive around a bit and think this over," he said, gunning the Capri's engine.

He drove at breakneck speed out New York Avenue

toward Route 50, then doubled back, taking the short, narrow streets near the Third Precinct by storm until he reached a side street a few blocks west of Union Station. Somewhere along the way he made two big decisions, one regarding the Browns, the other concerning his future. "Why postpone the inevitable?" a voice inside him had been asking for months, and he had no good answer for it. No more postponements, then—it was time to check out of the Hotel Grande for good, after he got the Browns situated. I-95 would be the best place for it.

"Why you got to drive so fast for?" asked Kimberly, breaking his train of thought.

"Job benefit," he explained, braking slightly. "I don't hold with the defensive driving thing."

Mid-way down the street he double-parked in front of the Hotel George, which sported a doorman and valet parking and looked fancy enough for them all to know they didn't belong there.

"Be right back—got some business at the hotel. Keep a low profile," he ordered and slammed the door shut.

"Brother-in-law in Richmond," the girl muttered as he left.

At length Jeffries emerged through the George's revolving door, loped across the street and motioned the Browns to get out of the car. "All right," he said, breaking a long silence, "to the Greyhound we will go, but not just yet. Quick—come with me," he ordered, grabbing mother and daughter each by the hand and steering them across the street into the hotel lobby. "I've already made all the arrangements. You two are staying in room 403 for the night."

"This—we ain't use to this kinda place, Detective. This is a little bit out of our, uh—"

"That's why I've got you staying here. Don't worry, Uncle Sam is footing the bill."

"For real?"

"For real. Now I don't want either of you to leave out the hotel tonight. You can order room service, or—"

"What's room service?" asked Kimberly

"You order dinner from your *room*," he said, "and they bring it there and *serve* it to you. Or if you want you can eat down in the restaurant, just be sure to charge the bill to your room number and they'll put it on my—on the tab."

"This place look pretty fancy to me," Mr. Brown allowed.

"Live a little," Jeffries advised, immediately regretting his choice of words. "I'll pick you up in the morning around five. Meanwhile, shower, freshen up, do all that woman stuff and be ready to take the bus to Richmond in the a.m."

"Well, we don't have anything to change to," Kimberly observed.

"Nothing I can do about that. They got robes in the room, maybe you can sleep in them tonight after you shower. I'll get a suitcase and you'll catch up with your clothes in Richmond. You want a full breakfast, same deal: order it to the room or eat down here, but *don't leave the hotel.*"

"Are we in that much danger?"

"No, you're ah . . . you're safe here. People are out there lookin' for you, to be sure, but no one would think of looking in this joint."

"I guess not . . . but . . . what's all this talk about Richmond?"

"I have a sister's in real estate down there. She'll find you a place to stay. Nice place."

"Is this some kind of witness protection thing like you was—"

"Exactly. Oh and I need to borrow a key to your apartment."

"Why?"

"Me and a friend are gonna do your packing for you. Don't worry, I won't mess with your stuff."

Ms. Brown looked at Kimberly, looked back at him, shook her head and tried to put the pieces together. Then she sighed and began fishing around in her purse for a house key.

"You'll find a couple suitcases under the bed. My bed," she said. Her eyes began to water and she turned away from him, still fumbling with her purse. As if turning would help her locate the key.

But he knew why she'd turned, and guessed her daughter did too.

"Here it is," she said, handing him a silver key. "You may have to jiggle it a bit. The door is—"

"Great. Now one more thing and we're done."

He left them, went over to the attendant at the registration desk, and returned minutes later with two plastic cards.

"You know how to use these?"

"What are they, credit cards?"

"No, they're like room keys, only plastic. Took me a while to figure that out too. My in-laws used to stay here when they visited, couple of centuries ago, when hotels had room keys. Now it's different: you'll see a metal box with a slot in it by the door handle, stick the card in the slot and pull it out fast. A green light will go on. Pull the handle and you can go right in."

"OK," said Ms. Brown, looking doubtful. "When you live on our side of the river, you don't go to places like this."

"It wasn't always this fancy, believe me. Anyway, you're

here now. Enjoy yourselves, get yourselves a good meal—and be up and ready to go at five in the morning."

"Five?" said Kimberly.

"I'm knocking on the door at five; all you got to do is be ready to go when you hear me. Got it?"

"We'll be ready," said Ms. Brown. "Thank you."

Jeffries turned abruptly and walked toward the hotel's entranceway. He looked back at them briefly, saw them standing there like gooney birds looking at the plastic cards, then made his way out to the street.

As he crossed to the Merc he flipped his cell open, poked a few buttons, and within seconds broke into a grin. The Baron, an old ne'er-do-well who owed him favors big time, had picked up. "Baron, it's Bad Dog. Glad to know you still walk among the living.... Yeah. Older, greyer, heavier. Hair look like steel wool after a scrubbing. I need your help tonight .... Been a long time, you still got the van? Great. Meet me at three a.m. at Benning and G; we're going to the Terrace to pack an apartment. Don't worry; I'll be there, armed to the teeth, and I'll help you load.... It's only one flight up. Naw, everyone will be asleep, trust me. You can make it, right?.... Right."

Jeffries figured if he grabbed some dinner and drove straight home—no, not home, he reminded himself, it wasn't a home, it was just a place he lived at—he could log about five hours of shut-eye before meeting up with the Baron. First he had to get in touch with his cousin Sheila in Richmond. Sheila was in real estate, and wouldn't be pleased when she heard what he wanted, but she was blood and one of the few relatives he could count on, in fact one of the few relatives he had, since his parents had been dead for years, his wife had—

"OK, stop it, don't *dwell* on it," he told himself. "*Enough.*"

But he couldn't stop the train of thought until his brain did the math on his daughter: it had been twenty-nine months and three weeks now.

V

As Jeffries walked toward the bus station later that evening he scanned the crowd and saw the usual gaggle of bewildered passengers outside, clutching their luggage and wondering where their buses were. He chuckled, remembering this was the new, improved Greyhound station, much better than the one they had demolished in the mid-'80s on K Street, known by the old-timers as the Ninth Circle—short for the Ninth Circle of Hell. On the inside, the Ninth was basically a collection of greasy tiles, carved-up wooden benches and broken lockers, made visible on occasion by flickering fluorescent lights. The exterior sported a cracked plastic "Greyhound" sign that no longer lit up, inspiring statements like "that dog ain't goin' nowhere," and a wraparound sidewalk littered with used needles, used condoms, bent spoons and cigarette butts. The walls were covered with so much graffiti no one could tell what color they were to begin with. The Ninth Circle was also a beacon for prostitutes and perverts; the former worked every alley and the latter lurked in every restroom. If all that wasn't bad enough, it was said more drugs were sold within the Circle's walls than bus tickets.

Checking out the new bus station, located on K Street a few blocks from Union Station, Jeffries could see it was patronized mostly by hard-working lower middle-class citizens without enough cash on hand to travel by air or even rail—folks like he grew up with in Northeast D.C. Closer inspection revealed a dealer standing on a sidewalk down the block, but he didn't see the usual loser's stew of con artists and petty thieves working the ticket lines inside. This was progress, he had to admit. But there were still a disturbing number of down-and-outers hanging around. They limped along in worn down shoes, wore bargain-basement striped shirts that hung loose over their raggedy jeans, and smoked like chimneys as if to pass the time. The men were a few days past clean-shaven, and both the men and the women had slick, shiny hair, so shiny it looked like it went a long time between washings. Most of these people were not criminals, he realized, looking more closely—no, they were unskilled, unemployed out-of-towners who had fallen on hard times. Refugees from areas rife with poverty. Maybe what the Browns would become if they went to Richmond with no money.

The Ninth Circle may have been hell, but its crew could afford its many vices because they could always get their hands on some easy green—there was money to be had if you wanted it bad. Now the buildings were brighter but the times were darker; you almost had to be a professional criminal to afford to raise hell or seek salvation the way the people did back then. As always, the down and out were beyond partying. They just hunkered down and worked the street, seeking only spare change and survival.

VI

Shortly after dawn the next morning, Jeffries pulled into the blacktopped parking lot outside the Greyhound station and motioned the Browns to get out. "OK, two tickets to Richmond. One way." He pulled two business cards from his pocket and thrust them at Ms. Brown. "This here's my card, don't lose it. The other one's for my sister. Her name's

Sheila McGee and she's a real estate agent. I called her; she'll be waiting at the station. She'll take you to your new apartment."

Ms. Brown took the cards and read them carefully. "Thank you," she said softly. "Why you doin' this, an' with your own money? I know it's your own money."

"Oh yeah, money," he said, and pulled a roll of bills from his pocket. The government paid the deposit and the first month's rent," he lied. "This here'll get you through the first couple a months."

"But . . . why? Why are you . . . ?"

"Hey. Gotta make sure you get to see your brother-in-law again."

She had to turn her head to the side for a moment to hide her embarrassment and get over that one.

"Just kidding. Peace of mind," he replied. "Jus' buying a little piece of mind is all . . . . You'll need to find a job, and get her enrolled in school right away. Can I trust you to do that?"

Ms. Brown and Kimberly both nodded.

"All right. To the Greyhound you go. But remember one thing. If this case goes to trial, I'm gonna—someone's gonna come get you wherever you are, Richmond or points south even, and bring you back to testify. You understand?"

"Yes sir," Kimberly replied.

Ms. Brown grimaced, but recovered quickly.

"I certainly appreciate you helpin' us get out of town, Detective," she said. "Don't you Kimmy?"

"If it saves us from gettin' shot, then yeah, I sure do."

"Richmond's not as far away as you think," he added. "It's less than two hours' drive down I-95. Lotsa gangsters go there to hide out, thinking it's the other side of the moon, but when the time comes we just send the marshals down there an' pick 'em up, easy as pie. Point is, don't be up here visiting cause if anyone sees you, they'll show up in Richmond after you get back, sure as shooting."

The three of them stood silently by the Mercury for a few seconds in the damp pre-dawn air. Then Jeffries shook their hands and said, "You better get going. Go directly inside and stay there until they start loading the bus. Gate five. And be careful in the station cause there's a few shady types in there—nothing special, just pickpockets, bus station riffraff and the like. If someone comes up to you, wants to sell you something, don't buy it. Keep the cash in your purse and don't let go your purse. When the bus comes and it's time to get on, don't just stand there in the wide open where who knows who's gonna lay eyes on you. You're not safe yet. The bus leaves in about a half hour."

"Detective—" Ms. Brown began.

"Later then," he said, opening the door to the Merc and lowering himself into its bucket seat. He revved the engine, slammed the door shut, and lowered the driver-side window. Then he pointed straight at the girl and said, "Kimba, you got a good mother there. Stick with her."

"I will," she said.

"Thank you so much," said Ms. Brown.

"You play any sports, Kimberly?"

"Naw."

"Hit the books then. You got some smarts," he said, tapping his head. "These kinda smarts. And . . . ."

"What?"

He felt his throat tighten and his tear ducts swelling, but he said it anyway: "Stay away from drugs. They'll kill you."

"I know."

"She knows that," added her mother.

Jeffries wanted to say more but couldn't face them any longer feeling the way he did. He didn't know how else to end it so he saluted them awkwardly, turned away from them and put the car in gear.

They watched him gun the engine, make a U-turn and pull out of the lot. The car whipped around the corner and disappeared within seconds. Ms. Brown extended her hand, as if to touch her daughter, but Kimberly moved away and the moment passed.

"Wonder if we'll ever see him again," the girl said.

As they walked side by side to the bus station, the first hint of light revealed itself in the east.

VII

A few minutes later Jeffries watched from his car as the blue-grey streaks of dawn fanned across the sky. Soon he saw glimmers of rose in the background, closer to the horizon. "Sky looks like a painting one minute and a big angry bruise the next," he mused. "Hell of a way to start the day, God."

He'd make the highway long before sunrise. He had visited Alicia's grave before meeting the Baron. Kissed the stone, touched the slab, almost shed tears he knew could not be drawn forth by anything else. Thinking back on it, he wished he'd left flowers on her grave. Tulips, she liked tulips.

He worked the Merc through traffic to D Street, then down the ramp to I-395, alternately braking and accelerating, changing lanes with aplomb. When he hit the tunnel, he shot right over to the fast lane. He powered out the south end of the tunnel at seventy mph, listening to the aging engine strain as he pushed it up the incline, then humming smoothly as it carried him down the dip in I-395 south just before it curved to the left, offering a view of the bridge over the Potomac. He loved crossing the 14th Street Bridge. The curve of the beautiful wide river soothed him, and there was something about the view of the city by the gleaming river, perhaps some quality of the Kennedy Center columns or the spires of Georgetown off in the distance, that made him smile—even if they were located in parts of the city he never got to, parts of it he saw only when crossing this bridge. He'd chosen this route in part because he wanted to take a last lingering look at the view.

Yessir, it was check-out time at the Big Hotel. He felt he was done. He was bowing out on a good note, astonished he'd actually helped some folks for once. Given himself a goodbye present of sorts. Goddam fortune to rent the hotel room, but so what? He was cashing in his chips anyway.

Several huge tanker trucks whizzed by him and he realized he'd fallen below the speed limit while catching the view. Once past the bridge, he pushed the pedal until the Merc hit eighty, promising himself he'd jump the median at the first opportunity. But when he saw the unbroken chain of concrete barriers dividing the north and south lanes, placed there to prevent exactly what he had in mind, he slammed his fist on the steering wheel repeatedly and swore. "Damn you, you picked the wrong road! No way to cross over!"

"OK," he reassured himself seconds later. "Don't panic, it's understandable. You don't sleep, you don't think straight." He hadn't slept as much as he'd intended—having spent most of the night with the Baron, packing the Browns' possessions.

Suddenly a northbound truck blasted by him. He winced at the slamming sound it made as it barreled by, felt the roaring wind in its wake, strong enough to pull the Merc to the left and just about suck its windows out, and rethought his approach. *Why take someone else with you on the way out? How selfish.* He'd seen the dead littering the highway at accident scenes before. It was always memorable but never pretty. He thought he'd had his escape all planned out, but it was turning into a big mess. Which was consistent with his entire post-Alicia life, so there was a certain logic afoot.

He nosed the car to the other side of the highway, thinking a better way out would be to veer into the arching cement wall of an overpass when there was enough distance between him and other drivers that he could be certain he wouldn't take anyone with him.

At length he found himself approaching the Duke Street exit. Its overpass fit the bill perfectly. He drew closer and closer, got ready to twist the wheel to the right when the time came, but the time came and went and he drove on and wasn't sure why. *Okay, just a practice run.* He would go full bore next time, pop a ninety-degree turn and make like a kamikaze into the next available wall. Meanwhile he found himself on a long straight stretch of highway, and a few miles later the yellow light by the speedometer blinked on: he was low on gas.

"What a damn fool," he said. "First man tryin' to kill himself on the interstate to run out of gas on the way."

He kept driving, knowing there would be a gallon left in the tank after the light went on, but couldn't help eyeing the needle on the gas gauge. There didn't seem to be an exit coming up any time soon. The needle was dropping fast, the yellow light was pulsing; he was approaching the moment of truth. He took a deep breath. His stomach was clenched and his hands gripped the wheel hard enough to bend it. Finally, another overpass came into view. It was about a mile away. He checked his rear view, edged into the right lane, unclasped his seat belt, and said, "Here we go."

He zipped past an exit sign, not bothering to read it, but then found himself easing the Merc to the right, onto the exit ramp, before reaching the overpass. He braked a bit but let the car's momentum push it up the ramp, which fed directly into a northern Virginia cross street loaded with traffic lights and barely moving vehicles. Soon he was driving in stop-and-go traffic, looking for a gas station, wondering if he'd be able to make one in time. By then he had to admit he wasn't going to do much more in the way of suicide the rest of the day.

He was waiting for a light to change when it crossed his mind he hadn't considered what to do with the Browns' mail. He pictured it piling up outside their mailbox. Another fuck up. What if they decided to return to the city to pick their mail up? Not a good idea. Maybe they wouldn't care—but what if there was a bill or a letter with a check in it? Something important they were expecting. Maybe he should have the P.O. forward it to Richmond—but then a bottom-feeder hot on their trail could go to the postmaster and learn their new address, and that would be that.

By now he was out of adrenalin and getting too sleepy to solve the problem. There was nothing to do except drive back to the District, call in sick, and try to rest up. A nap would clear his head; he'd figure the mail thing out later and then call Sheila. At the thought of Sheila, wearing her stylish real-estate agent pantsuit and showing the Browns around their new apartment, he almost teared up again. She was such a success.

Then came another disturbing thought: what if Carter's case did go to trial, and they couldn't find Kimberly Brown because he'd hidden her away in Richmond . . . and wasn't around to tell them where? On the other hand, if he told them now the rook would do something stupid, like send marshals to bring them back to town. So would King. There were so many details he hadn't thought through. Probably the thing to do was keep his trap shut and see how the case played out. If they indicted Carter and he pled, everything would work out. But then he'd have to stick around to find out which way things broke, wouldn't he?

Of course by this point he'd spent all his money, since he didn't think he'd need it anymore, and now he wasn't going to do himself in. Either he didn't have the nerve or he was too much like everyone else. Wanting to keep going, to keep on keeping on no matter how little sense it made. Truth was, the do-or-die moment had come and gone and he'd ducked and driven on. Simple as that. It was still OK if the inevitable happened, someone might get the drop on him one day, but apparently he couldn't get the drop on himself.

Anyway, now it seemed he had a lot left to do to make sure no one from either side of the fence would find the Browns before it was time for Kimberly to testify. He hadn't really wrapped things up at all. Maybe it wasn't such a bad idea for him to stick around, at least until he did. Odd feeling, having people to look after again. Not such a bad feeling either.

But for the moment he was just another cop with post-traumatic stress syndrome, stuck in traffic, hearing the honks and smelling the fumes. What remained of the Jeffries family, living out his days in the smoke and the haze. Poor Alicia. He found himself behind a bus, which reminded him of the one that had forsaken the Browns by the courthouse a million hours ago. He shook an unfiltered out of his cigarette pack and lit up. Took a deep drag and let the smoke out slowly through his nose. "Likely be the first person in the world to die from cancer of the nostrils. But what the hell, that'll come later."

He probably should check out the situation in Richmond in a week or so—make sure everything was working out. Make damn sure that sketchy teenager was getting her butt to school. Meanwhile, he would have to borrow some money just to make it through the month. He already owed Sheila the two months' rent.

He pictured the Browns in line at the bus station and smiled. The tears were about to come down, but he fought them off and drove on, through the northern Virginia traffic, looking for a gas station. They were never there when you needed them.

A Walk Down North Capitol Street

Imani was caught off guard by the news as she watched TV, preparing for bed. The reporter said the police found Santiago's body just before nightfall. He'd been shot down on Seaton Place, N.W. The detective said they'd responded to a 911 call from a man who said he saw the shots fired, but didn't give his name.

She sat down on the edge of her couch, stunned, and stared unfocused at the wall. Her eyes grew moist, but she didn't sob, she didn't move, she just sat and stared and let the tears roll down her cheeks. After a while she started to process what had happened.

The story on the TV was that Santiago had been gunned down by the Todd Place Crew for running numbers in Eckington, his old neighborhood up North Capitol Street. It was based on street speculation but made sense, because the shooting took place in the heart of the crew's turf. But Imani suspected the real shooters had driven across the bridge from Anacostia to do the job, on her former client Deonte Freeman's orders. After all, Santiago had gone to Lorton last Sunday to try to talk Deonte into calling off the hit he'd ordered on her after he'd been convicted. He blamed her for losing the trial because she'd refused to call his lying pal as an alibi witness.

Santiago had simply wanted to help her out, as he had so many times after she got him acquitted on that murder one beef. But while visiting Deonte, he managed to get into an argument with the youngster, who wound up threatening him. Santiago had shrugged off the threat, figuring he'd work things out with the blood down the line. But Deonte was a drug runner with a hot temper and evidently Santiago hadn't reckoned on his tendency to order hits on people who irked him.

Santiago was a street legend, but like her was also old school. These days the drug crews shot people just for staring at them, shot them as many times as it took. The streets weren't safe anymore, even for attorneys, which was one of the reasons she was thinking of giving the Public Defender Service notice and taking a break from the law for a while.

She knew most people thought Santiago was nothing more than a street felon with good survivor skills who'd done nine-tenths of what he'd been charged with. But what did they know, really? There was much more to him. Beneath his street persona lurked a heart with a soft spot for those he loved. He had saved her life twice—once on Orleans Place and once in an alley behind Fourteenth Street. He'd also tried his level best to help her out with Deonte, and even as her emotions peaked she saw he'd been gunned down for it. The realization cut deep: a legendary escape artist, known for not dropping his guard, had met his end trying to keep her alive. She lay down on the bed, drew a pillow close to her chest, and cried herself out cold thinking of him.

At four in the morning, it occurred to her she would have to attend his funeral sometime in the next few days. Then she realized she wouldn't be able to do that: too great a chance some unsavory type working for Deonte would recognize her, and to make fast money would either go after her solo or make a call to someone else who could.

She got up and trudged to the bathroom, glancing at the mirror long enough to see her corneas were crimson and her hair looked like a cornfield after a hurricane. Tomorrow — actually, today—was going to be a long day.

After wrestling with the idea until daybreak, she resolved to at least bear witness to the proceedings from somewhere near the parlor, the church, or wherever Santiago's service would be held. Maybe watch from a block or so away. Whenever a client died, even of natural causes, she went to the funeral. It was what you were supposed to do: see them through to the end.

* * *

Santiago's service was held the following Tuesday at the Mount Zion A.M.E. Methodist Church. The church was on North Capitol Street, just above Florida Avenue between Q and R. Imani knew it well from a case she'd won ten years ago, an armed robbery involving witnesses from the Unit blocks of R Street on both sides of North Capitol.

She checked out the area between New York and Florida Avenues from the back seat of her cab as it headed north, toward the church. Aside from a few signs of sure-to-fail gentrification near New York Avenue—sidewalk cafes were an ill-advised choice—things didn't look all that different from the way they'd been for decades, and for her money that wasn't a good thing. The housing was mainly red brick row homes in moderate to spectacular states of disrepair. Some were still single-family homes; others had been broken up into one-room apartments or rooms to let. Still others sat empty and abandoned, serving as hangouts for youngsters in the afternoons and havens for hoodlums at night.

The failed commercial strip on the block between Q and

R was anchored in the middle by the stone and mortar of the church. On either side of it the block was a jumble of barely open stores and boarded-up storefronts, connected by a cracked and heaving sidewalk. To the south of the church, down toward Q Street, Sly's Mini Mart did a trickle of business, and the stretch north to R Street boasted a pool hall and a liquor store. That was about it for commerce.

Several older men, seemingly worn down to fit the street, were drifting across the sidewalk to the curb, covering the bottles they drank from with paper bags, tastin' the drizzly afternoon away because they had nothing better to do. She knew these were men with no jobs and bad legs, too old for serious crime and without much in the way of family they were eager to get home to. Mainly what they had was each other and the broken-down block to hang out on until dark, when the neighborhood crews showed up.

As Imani's cab made its way up North Capitol toward the church she heard their lively exchange of epithets, catcalls and nicknames, all punctuated by laughter—and couldn't help but smile. The rain picked up a bit and the men began drifting back to the pool hall, where a back room crap game was surely in progress.

Another misty memory ran gently through her mind: she had gone in there once, trying to locate a witness; entered unannounced a room full of men gambling more for pride than money who did not want to be disturbed. It was early morning and the game had started the night before. The gamblers grumbled and swore, resenting the intrusion, although each one of them managed to give her a full-body eye frisk. She finally gave up and left, but one brother in his forties had followed her out to the sidewalk in the breaking light. There he told her the kid she was looking for was holed up a few blocks away, in a project called Sursum Corda, before asking her if she'd represent him on a burglary charge. She gave him her card and told him to call her and he smiled and thanked her and his gold incisor flashed in the morning sun. That was a long time ago and she was there today to pay her respects to him.

She took a moment while the cab sat for a light and tried to picture him. Imagine every feature of the grainy terrain of his face, in an effort to recapture what he looked like. So often she retained only a general image, closer to an impression cloaked in memory, of those who went down before her. She shut her eyes and focused on Santiago's graying hair, the patches of smooth, beardless skin on the scarred parts of his face, and his crooked-toothed smile parted by the shaft of gold.

His face had a weathered look, like he'd been out in the elements too long and too often during his fifty-nine years on the planet. She knew he'd been handsome once, but the tensions that came with a life of crime had left so many nicks and creases on his mug it looked like a roadmap. Like someone had taken an Exacto blade to sculpt the mask of a man marked by uncountable brushes with crime, violence and death.

It bothered her that when she first pictured him walking down the street, he was limping. Yes, there was a limp near the end, after the Park Police beat him, but for years his gait had been spry and jaunty. So she willed her way through the mists of months gone by to recapture a vision of him walking in the way she had always known.

She got out of the cab on R Street just above the corner of North Capitol. There she put on some dark glasses and an out of style hat with a wide brim, the sort of hat her mother would wear, and carrying a rolled-up newspaper walked up the block to an empty row house north of the church. She sat on its rusted wrought iron steps, knowing the view was partially blocked by a dying silver oak situated between the sidewalk and the curb. She opened the section of the paper containing the world news, spread it wide before her, and that provided the remaining cover she needed.

She wondered how many of Santiago's relatives would attend the service. She'd looked through her old case files and made some calls. It turned out he had kin in Richmond and in Southeast D.C., but not all of them had working phones. Or were still alive. His parents were long gone, but his brothers Matias and Martin, his Aunt Angela and his nieces and nephews planned to attend. He probably had a fair number of friends in D.C. but she had no idea if any of them would make the funeral. Some were locked up; some were on the run. She'd decided not to contact anyone other than his relatives: it was a good bet a blood he knew also knew Deonte had put a price on her head, so she'd left it to relatives and talk on the street to spread the word about the funeral.

She settled in only a few minutes before the mourners began arriving. People got out of vintage cars and walked up the street in twos and threes. The males wore black pants with white shirts. The flared edges of their black jackets peeked out beneath their coats. The women favored grey and black; the oldest still wore box hats with veils. She sensed Santiago's mourners knew all too well how to dress when paying last respects to kin whose lives had ended abruptly. They hugged and patted each other on the shoulders, then fell silent as they looked up the steps toward what lay in the gloom, beyond the massive open doors of the church. Then, having no other self-respecting choice, they straightened themselves up and went within.

The scene led her to think of her parents again and wonder how long they had to live. When would their funerals be held? She'd assumed they'd be held long before hers, but recent events suggested maybe not. She needed to get down to Georgia and visit them. It had been too long.

A few minutes later, a shiny black funeral parlor car double-parked in front of the church. Two young men jumped out and opened the shotgun-side door for a middle-aged, veiled woman who had to be Santiago's Aunt Angela. Imani figured the youngsters were her children. It started to rain harder and the tallest boy, a gawky teenager, held an umbrella over his mother's head and Imani began to tear up. She held the newspaper directly in front of her face and gave in to it. After a few seconds she regained control, lowered the paper, and fumbled her umbrella open. In the interval the family had gone inside.

A few late arrivals walked briskly up the steps. Then an usher in pinstripes appeared in the doorway, looked briefly up and down the street to see if there were any stragglers, and seeing none closed the thick wooden doors.

She hadn't been noticed. None of the mourners had even looked over at her, and since the press had finished feeding on the story of Santiago's demise days ago, there were no reporters in sight. She took her shades off, lowered the paper and sat staring at the door for ten or fifteen minutes, until her attention was drawn to an old woman pushing a cart down the sidewalk past the church.

The woman wore a navy watch cap and had bundles of clothing, a broom, and two or three knapsacks full of supplies in the cart. Imani figured her construction worker boots and bright blue Nordic vest had been given to her by one of the neighborhood shelters. She was having a difficult time lifting the cart up and over the curb to the sidewalk. The wheels wouldn't stay straight and it made her angry. It reminded Imani of the times she'd shopped with her brother using the same old messed-up carts. Eventually the woman got the cart over the curb and onto the sidewalk. She walked it on down the block toward Florida Avenue and was pushing it through the gas station on the corner when another distressed person entered the scene. This was an elderly stoop-shouldered man who shuffled up the street using a walking stick. He wore a jacket and tie and, having been caught in the rain without an umbrella, covered his head with a folded-over newspaper. Periodically he lowered his arm to his side and she realized the effort required to keep his arm up over his head, paper in hand, took more strength than he had. He got rained on for a bit, then lifted the paper to shield his head again, then lowered it and got rained on some more. He moved steadily up North Capitol, crossing R Street and continuing north toward Randolph.

After he disappeared from view she resumed staring at the church doors, thinking back on what Reverend Taylor, her Sunday-school preacher, had told her congregation decades ago:

"*We're all waiting for the same train, brothers and sisters. It's just a matter of when you get on board.*"

She sat through the service, thinking back on her escapades with Santiago over the years, until the church doors creaked open and about thirty people filed out. A shiny black hearse appeared a moment later; then six men carried the casket down the stairs and eased it into the vehicle. The black car reserved for family pulled up next. Aunt Angela and her children got into it quickly. It would be a sad thirty-minute ride to National Harmony Memorial Park, ten miles away in Landover. The mourners emerged from the church and moved toward several other cars lining up behind the hearse. Two of the younger pallbearers walked toward the hearse, shorn for the moment of any semblance of tough-guy street strut, and threw its doors open.

As they did so, a late model silver Mercedes drove up the street and double-parked in front of the church, motor running. Its occupants watched as the mourners continued filing outside and the casket was hoisted into the hearse.

A man looking to be in his mid-twenties emerged from the shotgun seat in the silver car and stood surveying the scene. Then he scanned the street, first looking south and then to the north, in Imani's direction. Suddenly he stopped still, straightened up, and looked directly at her. His eyes burned into her as if he knew exactly who she was. She cursed herself for taking her shades off, but held his gaze until he doffed his cap in her direction and slid back into his seat. The entire time he looked at her, her cheeks flushed and her heart tried its best to get into her throat. Did he know who she was? Or was he just acknowledging her presence and being polite? After all, she was looking at him too. She stood her ground as the driver gunned the engine, wondering whether and where to run, but then the car lurched forward and drove down the street, toward the Capitol. False alarm: its occupants hadn't come for her, they were just checking out the funeral.

Seconds later the other mourners' cars began pulling up behind the hearse, forming a line for the drive to the cemetery. Then the hearse pulled away from the curb, drawing the other cars behind it, and the caravan began moving toward Florida Avenue. There it turned left, following the path of the old woman with the cart, and like a freight train rounding a bend, moved slowly out of sight.

* * *

It was over. Imani left her spot in front of the house and walked without destination down the wide street the maps depicted as a red gash through the midsection of the city. In the clouded distance stood the white-domed Capitol building with the statue of Columbia atop it. Columbia faced east, as she had for over a hundred years, guarding the good citizens of her District from the British.

Everything she knew about Santiago's death she'd learned from two brief paragraphs in the *Post*. At first she didn't want to think about how it had happened: it was better not to be brought down lower by the details. But as she walked along it began to feel like he was walking with her, saying goodbye. She could hear his voice—perpetrator patter someone had called it—but it was more distinctive than that. He said things like, "If I was a horse, they'd a shot me by now," "Don't worry 'bout later till later come 'round," and in their last case together, "When I seen the one with the blade I sorta reacted by impulse."

As she crossed Florida Avenue, a stray thought slipping through her frazzled synapses suggested that after mourning him properly, she should say her goodbyes at the defender service, pack up her belongings, and set out for Georgia. That way she could visit her parents over Thanksgiving, and see how they were doing in their sixth decade. The English teacher and the career soldier who'd fought prejudice in the ranks as much as he'd fought his country's enemies. At least they had his army pension and owned their own house. Her brother Anthony was somewhere in Korea in uniform, so he wouldn't be there.

The weather was tolerable down home in winter, but fall was best. She remembered late October in Georgia: first frost, and suddenly she was a girl again, wandering through a field of peach trees with her parents at dusk, amazed. A few red-tipped leaves hanging on to the wind-swept branches, the rest fallen in close circles around each tree, lying limp on the browned grass, waiting for winter.

A block or two below Florida, which angled across North Capitol about a mile from the real Capitol, she entered junkie territory. "The junk," as her non-addicted clients called them, were out in force this rain-drenched afternoon. That didn't faze her. They were too strung out on horse to be violent and she was too preoccupied to care.

The late October wind picked up and a sudden gust kicked up an assortment of debris around her and blew her hat off. She tried to snatch it but it spiraled up and away from her outstretched hand. She stood watching as it blew topsy-turvy across the street, rolling aimlessly on its brim at times like some out of control wind-up toy, then jumping into the air again as if it had willed itself to fly. It soared upward for a moment, seemingly possessed by some kind of magical power to control its destiny, but it was only nature playing games; a moment later a downdraft sent it crashing to the pavement where it was immediately flattened by a passing sedan. Life on the street, she thought.

She retreated to a corner bodega on Bates Street to get out of nature's way for a moment, still wondering why she was, apparently, walking all the way home. Yellow, green and red lights flashed around the building's door. Why not call a cab? It would be easier—and safer. In the bodega she thrust dollar bills through an opening in the bulletproof glass in return for cigarettes. Then she was back on the street again, smoking a Kool down to its stub, pacing back and forth. She lit another one and inhaled, but before she could puff again a raindrop snuffed it out. She tossed the cig into the street, rubbed the rain from her face, swept back her frizzy hair, and began walking again. Her mind was a riot of random thoughts and feelings, racing from Santiago to Deonte to the tight, taut sensation she felt in her chest as she made herself take in every sight on every block in a neighborhood she'd spent so much time in over the years.

Was she really deciding, footstep by soggy footstep, to say goodbye to it all? It was Santiago's funeral to be sure, but for her it could also be—face it, girl—the goodbye tour of North Capitol Street. Goodbye to trolling for witnesses, checking out crime scenes, meeting shadowy figures in godforsaken locales to get leads on evidence no one else could find. She walked on, doing her best to avoid digesting the thought, through another block littered with junkies.

At New York Avenue she stopped and forced herself to take in the street scene once more. She saw evidence of horse, and also crack, everywhere she looked: a man with a fixed stare and open cut above his eye walked by her, bleeding what had to be HIV blood. Other addicts who had recently satisfied their habit followed him. They moved past her wide-eyed, like zombies, dreamy expressions on their scorched and scarred faces. Those who'd been unable to get their fix stood in doorways shivering, or jiggling their hands and feet, or doubled over; still others wandered down alleys and between buildings looking for a seller who might give them a boost on credit. The ones who'd already failed in that effort simply leaned against walls with dead eyes, jaws hanging and mouths drooling; they were beyond pain, beyond thought, gratefully numb to the sad chain of events that made up their lives. She surveyed the scene with care, taking in all the self-inflicted human misery, and asked herself why she'd ever thought she could make a dime's worth of difference in the lives of the poor souls staggering through that blasted landscape.

She wondered whether anyone in the white-domed Capitol building looming in the background wrestled with thoughts like these. White building, white people. Blocks away but another world entirely.

Her phone rang and, wondering who was calling, she yanked it out of her purse and stabbed a finger at the call button. The raspy-voiced caller wasted no time identifying himself.

"This Rocket. I work for Jamal Parker. You attorney Imani Jackson?"

"Speaking."

"OK, I work for Jamal, an' you don't need to know no more than that. He wanna retain you for his lawyer."

She stopped short and instinctively took on a more business-like posture, as if doing so would make up for the fact she was lawyering on a city sidewalk in the rain.

"I think I know what the charge is, right?" she asked.

"Yeah, murder one, you know, but JP know you a good lawyer an' when he seen you got Rashon Burns off, he know you ain't soft, you see what I'm sayin'? You a woman but you hard as a lawyer, you know?"

"I guess I know what you mean. I'm not . . . soft," she said evenly.

"He say he pay a hundred thousan', fifty thousan' before the trial an' the rest after."

"I'm with the Public Defender Service, so I can't take a pay case."

"OK but can't you get them to let you take the case anyways? It's a big case—I mean, that's the game, an' you in it, right?"

"That's the game," she replied, dodging the question. "Where is he?"

"He come by your office tomorrow afternoon, say two o'clock, with his posse. He on bond—half a million.... You in, right?"

She didn't answer right away. Instead she gazed across the pothole-cratered street, past the shattered glass, past the dazed and broken figures slumped against the crumbled buildings on the far side—gazed past it all, trying to imagine herself living a different kind of life in some peaceful tree-lined locale. It was hard to picture.

"Did you know a brother named Santiago?" she asked.

"Naw."

"He was a former client of mine. He's dead now. He was a—"

"Look, what up?" Rocket demanded. "I don't care 'bout no dead men."

As she took in Rocket's reply the silver Mercedes from the funeral sped through the forlorn landscape, windows down, blasting the very air around her with decades-old lyrics from Public Enemy: *"I'm ready and hyped, plus I'm amped/Most of my heroes don't appear on no stamps,"* or maybe the lines were from Welcome To The Terrordome, she wasn't sure, but either way the burial service was clearly over and the young toughs were roaring down the street, more determined than ever to drive fast, live hard, and leave their mark on life.

"I'm sayin', *what up*?" repeated the Rocket impatiently. "I mean he innocent, man—the brother who snitched on him got, like, no respects for the truth, I swear to God."

"I can't help you, Rocket. I may be leaving the Defender Service—in fact, leaving the city. Tell Mister Parker I wish him the best."

"What?"

"Take care now."

She hung up and put the mobile phone back in the bag, her hand shaking.

"Damn," she said. "Parker's a big, big fish . . . and there I go tossing him back in the sea. Guess I really am leaving it all behind."

Funny, she thought, gazing back across North Capitol. Get a hundred junkies off scot free or into rehab and nobody notices, but get one major crime figure like Jamal Parker off and the whole world turns its attention in your direction, captivated, and you're in the headlines. In the last few years she'd been in the headlines more often than she wanted. It was the nature of her cases. Public Defender Service attorneys always got the big bad felonies, the ones reporters followed like bloodhounds.

She felt a sudden letdown. It was clear she was done trying cases for quite a while, maybe forever. She shivered. Maybe it was excess emotion working its way through her body or maybe it was the weather. In the last twenty minutes the sky had turned a notch or two toward evening. The temperature had fallen and the rain had tapered off to a point where the drops left her more chilled than damp. She looked around and noticed there were fewer people on the street. It was rotten weather and getting on toward dusk, so no wonder she felt morose. But it was more than that. She should have taken the case, she thought for a fleeting second. Stay on for a while longer. But the next moment she told herself no, saying no was the right thing to do. Even Santiago had told her leaving made sense.

She began walking again, finally drawing closer to the safer, more integrated part of North Capitol—the part framed by high-rise buildings, small well-kept parks and, in the middle distance, the burnished brick buildings of Gonzaga High School.

She stepped off the curb to cross M Street, failing to notice a beat-up Buick run the light until it sideswiped a car halfway through the intersection. She registered the thud and the screech and watched amazed as the Buick spun 180 degrees before the brakes kicked in and the driver was able to regain some kind of control. He hit the gas, turned the smashed vehicle back around, tires squealing all the while, and raced up the road—leaving the other car sitting in a collage of broken glass, shards of chrome and foul blue-green liquids leaking from its underbelly. It was pure North Capitol Street theater.

It all happened in seconds, and as it was crossing her mind that if the Buick had hit the other car a nanosecond earlier it would have been a free trip to the morgue for two, the silver Mercedes threaded its way through the intersection, heading north now, and a sense of dread wafted through her mind. Third sighting—either they were drag racing North Capitol for the pure sport of it, or they were looking for someone, and her sinking heart whispered it might be her. The car had slowed down for a moment, but then raced off toward the church, so maybe they hadn't seen her. Maybe she'd been just another figure in the blurred background as they zoomed by. Thank goodness she was no longer wearing the floppy hat. It stood out. They would have remembered it and done a U-turn.

But U-turn or not, if they were searching for her they might come back. The thought prompted her to turn and walk east on Pierce Street, as quickly as she could without slipping or breaking into a dead run. She headed for the corner of Pierce and First Street N.E., knowing it ran parallel to North Capitol, angling down toward Union Station. She'd worn sneakers, but by now her feet were smarting and the canvas scraped her heels like sandpaper.

Once at the corner, she moved back from the street toward the front entrance of an office building. The building was closed, but its overgrown hedge would hide her from searching eyes should the occupants of the silver coupe drive by. She stood panting and coughing in the brick walkway, vowing to give up smoking. She caught her breath, moved closer to the building, and was soon shielded by the hedge and a clump of wilting arborvitae.

The pungent smell of the mulch circling the shrubs led her to picture Santiago's burial in her mind's eye. The ceremony, the mound of fresh brown dirt, his remains swallowed whole by the ground. The mourners drifting away. Even as the scene slipped through her mind, it registered with her that not many relatives or friends would be there to help her if she were shot and survived—or, if she died, to pay their respects when she got to the last stop on Reverend Taylor's train.

It was a good idea not to tell her parents about any of this. The less they knew the better, at least for the moment—but she would spend some time with them as soon as she could. Catch up, listen to their old LPs, put some distance between her and the life it seemed she could no longer live, and recharge. Lay back in Albany, GA and think everything over. She had done her bit. She had tried her best. Yes, it was time to lick the wounds and move on. As the old gospel song said:

"You got to move, you got to mooove
When the Lord says ready, whoooo – you got to move."

She waited behind the bushes for about ten minutes, but saw no sign of the silver Mercedes. It was getting darker, and darkness made the bad neighborhoods bordering North Cap even worse. She looked around for a cab. There were none in sight, so after another scan for safety's sake, she emerged from her leafy hideout and walked briskly down the street, toward Union Station. She had paid her respects—to Santiago, to the crime-ridden city, to her many clients—and remained fully intact. Now it was time to move on.

Loveboat

James Spaulding was lying on his bunk, watching the purple dots cross the wall and wondering how he was ever going to get back to D.C., when a buzzer sounded and the door to his cell slid open. Seconds later Eddie Proctor walked through it, carrying a dinner tray in one hand and a rusted bedspring in the other.

"Don't even bother," Proctor said as Spaulding rose and did his best to assume a defensive posture. "Let's see you box with this, man. The tip is razor-sharp, so your face gonna look like a roadmap when I'm done. Which is what you get for hurting a child like you did."

For a second, Spaulding harbored the hope that what he was experiencing was only the dark side of a PCP flashback. Surely the guards hadn't placed him in solitary to protect him from Proctor, and then detailed Proctor himself to serve dinner to the solitaries. Even they weren't that stupid—it was a flashback, right? Wrong, another part of his mind replied as Proctor stood grinning before him, dinner tray in one hand and blade in the other. Wrong, it said again as the homemade shiv flashed before his eyes: the nightmare vision was real, and there was no room to run in the ten-by-twelve foot cell.

"Thought you could save your sorry self by hiding in solitary, didn't you," said Proctor as he dropped the tray on the desk between them.

Spaulding caught a whiff of mashed and mixed vegetables, but wasn't about to check out the particulars. Sensing his foe was about to make his move, he grabbed the tray and thrust it upward so its contents splattered Proctor. Then he adjusted his stance to ward off the attack he knew was coming.

Proctor didn't pause to wipe away the steaming glop that covered his face and body. Instead he lunged at Spaulding and jabbed the shiv at his stomach. Spaulding countered with the tray, parrying the thrust with the hard plastic rectangle. Proctor lunged again, Spaulding wielded his plastic shield, and so it went for what seemed an eternity: thrust and parry, thrust and parry. A fight to the death but at the same time, in Spaulding's freewheeling, PCP-drenched mind, a boxing match of sorts. Drug addict that he was, he still considered himself a boxer, and while he wouldn't have lasted two minutes in a real ring, a combination of instinct and adrenalin kept him on his feet in this fight, which lasted just long enough for the guards to get to the cell, grab Eddie Proctor and stomp him to the floor.

Evidently they had made a lot of noise. Still, Spaulding figured—in the brief paranoid moment before it was his turn to taste the nightstick—it was hard to believe the sound of plates and cups crashing to the floor, even combined with their grunts and curses, could have carried all the way to the guards' station. Must be hidden speakers, he told himself, yeah that was it, but what did it matter? The turnkeys had been mobilized, and once mobilized they did not wind down easily.

After unleashing a volley of body shots on Proctor, they turned their attention to Spaulding. One guard tackled him; the other ripped the tray from his hands and split it in two over a chair back. He covered his face, and assumed a fetal position while the guards rained nightstick blows on his head and back.

"All right you sonofabitch, what happened in here?" the senior officer asked Spaulding. He couldn't muster an answer, so after some high-intensity grumbling and threatening, the guards dragged Proctor out of the cell and closed the door behind them.

Spaulding remained in a heap on the floor. He felt like he'd been stung by a squadron of bees. Just keeping his eyes open felt like heavy lifting. But soon he noticed a small green broccoli floret, floating with some other food scraps in a pool of water inches from his nose. The tiny floret was cut in the shape of an evergreen. He had always loved trees, so wasn't surprised when the image of a real evergreen, standing tall and proud in the forest, flashed before his eyes. But seconds later he saw it crash to the woodland floor, felled by an axe—much like he had recently fallen to the concrete floor, felled by nightsticks. He wasted no time concluding he was the human version of the tree: a tall, proud being, damaged and brought low.

It struck him then just how far he had fallen in the past forty-eight hours. Higher than a kite on Loveboat, he'd set in motion an incredible series of events—events that resulted in his arrest, incarceration, and—now—prostration. Sprawled on the floor of a cell in the Baltimore City Jail, freedom a thing of the past, he knew he'd fallen as low as it was possible for a human being to fall. The thought pressed in on him and was unbearable. He felt like crying but forced himself not to, fearing a shuddering cry would bring him more pain than release.

Instead he closed his eyes and waited, hoping for sleep and the peace of dreams. He was rewarded with both in short order. While dreaming he saw himself as a child again, still blessed with his father's favor. He was climbing to the top of a hickory tree, high above the earth, feeling connection with all things as he surveyed an endless blue sky around him. He was back in the days of wonder and promise.

He woke to wonder where that promise had gone, to remember the dream, and—still on the floor, watching the floret float in the pool of bloodstained water before him— resolved to put his life in order. *I can still do it,* he thought. Soon, he would be standing free in the open air again, an upright being filled with hope. But a second later a surge of activity in his spinal cord set off a series of spasms in his arms and legs, and after regaining control of them he abandoned his commitment to reform.

The straight and narrow path to daylight and freedom? Sure, right, snickered the voice in his drug-soaked prefrontal lobes.

Besides, even if he tried, wouldn't life gang up on him big time, like it always did? Hadn't his heroes turned on him? Wasn't all existence unfair? And the kicker was, none of this was his fault! Like this kidnapping thing everyone in the dorm got so *riled* about on day one: when he'd tried to explain why he took the toddler, everyone turned on him, with Proctor the Dorm Lord leading the charge. Then again, Proctor was no worse than the police. How many times had he told them? He was only trying to teach the girl's mother a lesson: watch out for your kids, Tanya. She kept letting the little one, Latisha, roam away. Mom was too easily distracted, way too country for the city, should have stayed in that crud-rusted trailer up on blocks in Cecil County.

"All I done," he told himself, "was try to get her to see what could happen if she let her child roam around too much. I mean someone could come and snatch the child right off the street—and I showed her how it could happen, but just as a warning. Tell me how that's kidnapping and abuse!"

Looking back on it, he realized he should never have come to Baltimore. It was a bad idea—in fact it was a PCP-induced day trip. But two days ago, after he'd found Tanya and her child wandering the cracked and crumbling streets of the city, he'd done a good thing: taken them in and fed them. Missed gym time to take care of—and that was another thing! The boxing! So what if his father didn't like it! "Hanging out at the gym, thinkin' you're big time, get a job." What, at the Post Office? Didn't seem to do much for the old man; he looked more licked than the stamps.

Incensed by these thoughts, Spaulding began shouting, as if his father stood stooped beside him in the cell. "Can't fight, huh? Shoulda seen what I just done to Proctor!" he raged.

There was no response, but the flash of anger left him with enough energy to drag his legs closer to his rump, hoist his battered body up on its left elbow, and work his way to his feet. Holding on to his bunk to steady himself, he surveyed the cell. It was a mess, just like his life.

And yet the whole caper still made sense to him. Nothing bad could have happened to the girl, really. She'd been safe, he'd seen to it. Not only that, he'd shown her a great time. First they'd had a fantastic ride down Gardeners Hill, eighteen-month old Latisha gooing and cooing the five blocks to the light. He could hear every sound she made because he'd had her tucked in close to his chest, football style. His right arm around her, her head firmly in his hand, he'd raced all the way down the hill. No way was he going to drop her! And his left hand was free to steer, which was fine because it wasn't like a ten-speed took two hands for steering. Besides, they were barely going thirty. Maybe forty after a while. But it was fun! A four-minute mile on a forty-five degree angle, the baby smiling as the traffic rushed by. Speeding downhill, the wind whistling by, they were invincible!

And the rooftop of the Holton Arms apartment building was a great choice. No one would find her there, no one except the mighty Spaulding, who—because the plan was, once Mom realized the error of her ways, he would escort her to the roof, produce the child unharmed, and say *see! Don't you ever let this young smiling beauty out of your sight again. It's neglect! Look what could happen!*

At least that was what he'd intended, til he'd seen that astonishing view from the rooftop. He and Latisha had been transported. Sitting on the ledge, above the tenth floor, the air so clear and an incredible view of the neighborhood spread wide before them. For a while there, he thought he might fly—or at least drift slowly through the air—to get back down. Why do those stairs again? Flying didn't seem like it would be that hard to do, but then the drug had its own logic and he'd changed his mind before flexing his wings. Decided they should simply sit there, taking in the view. It was a while—way too long, really—before he realized the squad cars they'd been watching were converging on the street below them. Oh yeah and the helicopter, he hadn't seen that coming either. The Loveboat was a trip, but sometimes it made things sneak up on you that you should have seen coming for miles.

Still, it was great stuff while it lasted, it made you feel—powerful, no—omnipotent! Something bubbled up briefly inside him, and he smiled the smile of the all-knowing, even now, a few days after his last hit. Seemed like his father's dire warning about how the stuff got into your fat cells and stayed there for months was true. The smile became a grin that spread throughout his entire body, softening it, making it easy for him to slide to the floor. When he got there he closed his eyes, watched the purple dots do their dance inside his eyelids, and passed out again.

He woke thinking he was at a beach and had fallen asleep in the sun. "Stupid thing to do," he said, covering up, but then the sun became a floodlight and he remembered where he was. The lights were always on in solitary, so for all he knew it was the middle of the night. On the other hand, it was beyond dispute he'd been out cold for a good stretch, long enough to wake up aching. The guards, he remembered, fingering his head wound carefully. An image of them on their knees, begging him for mercy, zipped through his head. At least the bleeding had stopped.

He started to get up off the floor, then froze as he heard footsteps coming down the hallway. A hot flush of fear flooded his body. Was it Proctor, on a return trip to finish the job? Or the guards, on a similar mission? He listened, blood pulsing through raised veins, as slow, heavy footsteps passed by the door and faded into the surrounding silence. No, he decided, this wasn't paranoia. It was fear based on reason. Which meant the PCP had receded further into his fat cells, leaving what remained of his brain in a state closer to sanity than lunacy. A thinking man's distance from the highs and lows of recent mind trips. The drug tide was receding, leaving its residue to be sure, but for the moment he was able to ponder his predicament with a semblance of rational thought.

And what a predicament it was. Proctor would be out of commission for a few days, recuperating. But there were others who wanted his blood. Proctor's pal Eugene Bowe, awaiting trial on a murder beef, had promised to crush Spaulding's windpipe with his bare hands if he caught him alone. And Tyler Carson, a/k/a Carcinogen, violent enough to be held in preventive detention, spit at Spaulding whenever he saw him. Others, too—no matter how many times he told them he'd meant no harm to the girl, indeed that she'd escaped unscathed.

It was purely and simply a matter of the code, a code devised and enforced by the inmate culture, a code that condoned all crimes save those against a child. Why, he didn't know. But he found himself wondering what sort of childhood had produced Bowe and Carson's great concern for the well-being of children.

All of a sudden he saw Carson's frightening face in the corner of the room. He closed his eyes and the face went away, but soon it was replaced by a strange sort of movie: *Assault on Mount Spaulding*, a film projected by his mind on the inside of his eyelids. One on one he was able to stave off his attackers, using left and right hooks, but then they combined forces, came at him in a pack and tore him apart. Seconds later he saw himself whole again, in prizefighter mode, beating them back. Saving his skin, repelling them all with swift, accurate punches. But in another moment he saw himself on the floor, cowering as they set upon him with steel pipes, and he realized there was only one way to avoid making the movie a real-life event: swallow hard, call the old man and ask him to post his bail money. Making the call wasn't going to be easy, but survival was a big motivator. He tried to think things through, consider his options, and decide. In the process, he dozed off again.

Later that morning, he managed to get permission from the guards to call his father and beg him to pay the fifty thousand dollar bond the lockup judge had laid on him. He knew it was morning because while he'd slept a plate of scrambled eggs, a carton of milk and an orange (plastic spoon, no tray thank you) had appeared in the cell.

The turnkeys, a different set this time, said nothing as they escorted him to the drab room where the phones were installed. They left him there alone to make the call. Spaulding knew it was an open question whether his father would be willing or able to put up the money, and his chest tightened as he dialed the black rotary phone he'd been given to access the outside world. He wondered how many other inmates, now possibly dead, had used the ancient instrument to make similar calls over the years.

He dialed and listened to the hollow ringing sound he knew so well, figuring he'd hear it at least ten times before anyone got to the phone. Then he heard his father's trademark hello, delivered in a flat voice tinged with sadness.

"Pop, this is James. I'm at the Baltimore Jail. The one on Eager Street."

"I know where you are, son," said Amos Spaulding, and the air went dead for a beat.

"Look, I need to ask you for a favor. I need help gettin' out of here; they trying to kill me."

"Who is it, the guards?"

"No, it's the brothers I'm locked up with. Just some of them. One of them, mainly."

"It only takes but one," was the considered reply. "Fifty thousand dollars" was his father's next utterance.

"I know, it's a lot of money."

There was a sigh, one in a series stretching back decades, and Spaulding could picture his father rubbing his forehead, as if to smooth away the pain.

The older man cleared his throat and said "I get the money, I'll post the bond on one condition. Your mother found a in-patient drug treatment facility called Truth House that you can go to. It's just over the D.C. line, and I'm willing to mortgage the house to raise the money if you agree to go there."

"What do you mean, in-patient?" asked Spaulding. As if he didn't already know.

"It means just what it says," came the retort, "you go *in* there for a few months, as a *patient*, an' get that rat-poison out your system." Then, calmer: "They got counselors, therapies an' doctors. It's liable to cost goin' on five thousand dollars in addition to the bail money an' if you up an' leave, I don't get none of it back. Been thinkin' about it since before you called. Spoke to the lawyer about it yesterday and she thought it was a excellent idea. So does your mother."

It made sense to Spaulding that his mother had found the drug clinic—given her lifetime love affair with alcohol, she knew the rehab circuit better than Dr. King knew the road to Birmingham—but he rejected the idea outright. "What's the point," he heard his voice echo in the room, "I do all that an they'll still put me in jail the minute I get out."

Another sigh preceded the reply. "No, I talked to the lawyer 'bout that, son. The idea is to line you up a job while you're in there, so by the time you go back to court for sentencing, you're employed *and* drug-free. She thinks you got a shot at probation, you do all that. Being as how you're a first offender and all."

Spaulding snorted. "Sounds like the lawyer usin' PCP too."

"Well, my own self I'd be inclined to throw the book at

you on account of there was a child involved, but she seems to know what she's doin' so I don't know."

"Damn," Spaulding exclaimed, "I'd have to be a whole different person to do that!"

"That's the point!" his father began yelling. "You better become a whole different person *fast*, or you're done for! Hurting a young child like that!"

"I didn't hurt her, matter of fact I was—"

"Lucky, that's what you was! Think what you'd do if it was your own child! You'd want to kill the man who messed with it! But you'd have to be a father to understand that, so I guess you never will."

"Pop—"

"You can't go on like this! An' don't tell me how you're gonna go back to boxing. Boxing's over! It's time you started thinking 'bout someone besides your own self an' settled down."

There was a silence, punctuated by Spaulding's heavy breathing: the diatribe had left him shaken. Just hearing his father speak the words *settle down* was enough to set his teeth on edge, and the man hadn't stopped there. He was about to slam the phone down when he heard the sounds of other voices in the distance. The calm, fun-filled, barely audible voices of children. They were coming from the receiver; somehow, other conversations had been spliced into their circuit. Probably, he thought, from some parallel universe where people like him weren't allowed.

But hearing the children's voices soothed him, and when his father asked, "What do you say, son? I can still prob'ly get you a job at the Post Office," his reply was soft and even: "I can't do it Dad, it's not me. I'm gonna hang up now."

He put the phone down and sat there fingering the buttons

on his jumpsuit, wishing Bowe and Carson would appear and make short work of him.

Settling down struck him mostly as another way to die. Whenever the words were uttered, Spaulding pictured sediment drifting slowly to the bottom of the ocean, like it did in high school films about how it took ten thousand years for protozoa to turn into oil. "Slow death in life or fast death in prison," he snorted, then found himself wondering if he'd become the wretch he was simply to give the old man something to rage about. A gift of sorts, to stir his father's passion, wake him up, rattle his cage.

"But so what," he muttered, "I get the man cookin', all he does is ask me to roll over and live his kinda life."

The Post Office Life was one his father had suggested many times before. As Spaulding knew, it was a life marked and bounded by the twin pillars of routine and duty. An easy-going, predictable life measured out in paychecks and pensions, TV shows and TV dinners. Even in his current state, Spaulding knew he couldn't settle down to that.

Part of him still wanted to be a boxer. Or a fireman, a medic, a pilot. Even a tree-trimmer, if the trees were high enough. Someone who risked death and courted danger, so had to be alive and kicking at all times. Someone incapable of standing behind a Formica counter hours at a time, shifting his feet and muttering "next." Sure, fighting for his life in prison was terrifying—Proctor was death with clothes on—but it felt real. The stakes were high and that made him feel strong, focused and clear-headed. He felt fully alive; energy pulsed and crackled inside him. Every moment counted, precisely because it could be the last.

Maybe, he thought, he should ride things out in the Big House and see what happened. After all, he'd bested Proctor and could probably whup them all, one on one. Yeah, maybe it was time for a new Dorm Lord. Could be a title fight after all, followed by his crowning as the new champ. A short, violent reign and then permanent retirement, most likely. Not much really and yet everything he'd longed for—just in a different arena.

As he sat by the phone, waiting for the guards to lead him back to solitary, he noticed a wave of tiny newborn spiders inch out of a crack in the moulding and make their way into the box-like room. No doubt Momma S. rested nearby, spent from spawning the tiny creatures already bent on fleeing her. No, he corrected himself, they weren't fleeing her; they were embarking on a courageous journey, going out to meet the world head-on. And what was that world populated by? People like him. "If they only knew," he mused, grinning. Still, the journeys of these little critters—from the dark cradle of their nest, up and across institutional green walls and onto the uncharted ceiling of their universe, seeking a spider's light and truth—struck him as worthy of respect. They were gambling with their six-legged lives, and he liked that.

He noted that for once in his life he held a position of great power. He could aid the spiders in their journeys or stamp them out of existence forever. He had never much liked spiders—the sight of them full grown and close made him shiver—and was tempted to take a moment and wipe them all out. Cute now, but man, so *butt-ugly* when they grew up. Besides, weren't most of them destined to be stomped, smeared, or sprayed anyway?

But then his eyes were drawn to one of the spawn in particular. This one—male or female? Boy or girl? Spider or Spidah? he wondered—was obviously headed for the door. He watched as it climbed assorted barriers, on a dead run for what . . . the keyhole! Half an hour old and making its run for daylight! He sat there cheering the little fuzzball on until it disappeared inside the hole. Escaped, gone, made it. Christopher hairy-legged Columbus, gone fishin' in the New World. He wished the creature well, then sat back and closed his eyes for an oddly emotional moment.

For a second he worried he'd see spiders under his lids, crawling by and freaking him out, so was relieved to see what appeared instead: the perfectly harmless picture of a young child playing pool. It—the kid—was lining up a stick, about to take a shot. No surroundings, just the kid and the pool table. The kid took the shot, the balls tore across the table, the other player appeared and it was . . . him. It dawned on him that the child was his child, and they were playing pool together. No big emotions, no conflict. He was simply playing a game with his child.

But he had never thought of himself as a father before. Always viewed himself as the one to be cared for, not the caregiver. Was the child with the cue stick a boy or a girl? Too late, the image was gone. But he trembled in its afterglow, knowing what it signaled. His father's words—"think what you'd do if it was your own child!"—ricocheted through his mind and in a second he crumpled forward, squeezed tight by huge racking sobs that erupted from somewhere deep in his body. Soon hot tears ran through the creases in his contorted face.

After he regained his composure, he checked out the wall positions of the baby spiders again. They hadn't moved much, and he wondered if they'd been shocked still by his crying. Thank goodness his jailers hadn't seen him. But where were they anyway? Had they forgotten him? Would he remain in the phone room until they brought down another prisoner and noticed their error? Or had they left him here on purpose, for Bowe or Carson to find?

The latter possibility weighed on him, and rather than entertain it in any depth he longed to be unconscious again. He tried to drift off, but couldn't manage it, having slept through most of the last day. That left him thinking more about the child at the pool table. Was the poolroom vision just one last drug-induced mind trip? No, the 'Boat trip was over; the baseless fears, spinal surges and sudden shakes were gone, replaced by a constant dullness that drifted through his head like cloud cover, casting shadows on his thoughts and visions. He found himself thinking rational thoughts again. Yes, the fog was lifting, but what was being revealed? Nothing less than the true nature of his latest escapade. The reality of it now loomed before him, undeniable and pathetic, no longer translated via drug magic into a tale of justification told by an innocent. Yes, the enormous stupidity of what he'd done was becoming clear. And yet, didn't it all start out as an act of responsible fatherhood? An erstwhile effort to give a mother a parenting lesson?

It had, but as recent events had revealed, parenting wasn't for those who thought they could take their children flying without a plane. Face it; he was an addict, just like his mother. Would anyone who knew him be willing to bear his child or marry him? What would he do for work to support wife and child—make license plates in prison, paint halfway-houses in his later years? Spaulding as parent and breadwinner—it was a laugh-out-loud notion unless he changed completely and learned to embrace the sort of necktie life he'd heretofore resisted. Could he do it for the sake of the pool-playing phantom he had just imagined? Did he really want to do it?

It was an impossible idea, really. But then why did the image leave him short of breath?

Suddenly the door slammed open and the appearance of a linebacker-sized guard put an end to his musings. He hadn't seen this one coming, and didn't know what to expect until the words "stand up, motherfucker" rang out and the possibilities became clear to him. He rose and snapped to attention, eyes to the floor.

"I heard about you," the guard observed as he circled him. Spaulding said nothing, realizing the phone room was a place where trouble might well go unnoticed. "You know I use' to be a drill instructor in the Corps," the turnkey continued, "and I was fair but when tough guys like you gave me a hard time I would *respond*, know what I mean?"

The name Aikens appeared in white print on the guard's black plastic name tag. "Look, Mr. Aikens," said Spaulding, "I don't want no trouble. If you're gonna hit me, go ahead an' hit me. Get it over with."

"You want me to hit you?" the guard inquired.

"No, but I ain't gonna beg you not to."

The response gave the big guard pause. "You got more balls than most junkies," he observed finally.

"That's 'cause I'm not a junkie," Spaulding replied despite himself.

"Right, an' I'm not standin' here neither," replied the guard, grinning. Then he began to laugh, and to make small talk as he patted Spaulding down, and they both relaxed.

As Aikens steered him through the metal maze leading back to solitary, Spaulding realized the futility of his recent longings. *Just like me to get thinkin' about children without having a clue who their mother might be. Most men would find themselves a woman an' fall in love first.* But there he was, locked in limbo with no one to call. Small wonder—most of his love interests had backed off once they realized he was into drugs, and he'd managed to infuriate the rest. No, there wasn't a woman on the planet he could call, not even Tanya. Come to think of it, *especially* not Tanya.

Back in his cell, he wondered how he had reached this state of affairs. He wasn't a daily user, but he'd become a frequent flyer and that didn't leave a lot of energy for relationships. The focus was totally on satisfying his own needs: getting high, laying low, paying for the habit.

"Truth is," he told the walls, "ridin' the Loveboat don't leave you much time for love." Viewing things from this perspective, he realized he'd been living in solitary long before he landed in the Big House. Then his father's admonition sailed back into his head: *"Start thinkin' about someone besides your own self an' settle down."* The words hurt more this time because he realized the man's point: settling down involved others, and that was its draw.

These thoughts roiled around in Spaulding's head and led him to a sad conclusion: what a self-centered fool he was! How ridiculous of him to think about starting a family. He'd have to make some big changes to go down that road. Big, big changes. The first would be to get off the 'Boat for good. Then get a job, some money, and . . . good God, what was he thinking about? Next thing he'd be signing in at a drug treatment program.

Later that night, he found himself struggling once again to achieve a state of sleep. He was on the brink, drifting, when the clash of sounds that signaled the unlocking of his door began.

"Got a court hearing this morning, Spaulding," boomed Aikens. "Got to be fed, dressed an' on the court bus by four a.m. Bond review motion... what's a matter, you don' like it here in Heartbreak Hotel?"

Spaulding answered with a grunt, which only made Aikens laugh. "Someone be here in a minute to feed you, then I'll take you to the bus," said the chunky guard as he withdrew his key from the cell door. "I'm gonna leave this open for the food detail while I go wake Mr. Youngblood down the hallway; call me if you need me."

Spaulding stood blinking in the harsh light, trying to figure out what he had to do to get ready for court. Soon he realized that since he'd slept in his clothes, putting on his shoes and socks was all that was necessary. He edged an unsteady foot into a laceless shoe, his mind racing as he considered the possibilities. Evidently Miss Rothenberg had filed a motion seeking his release before trial, and the judge had agreed to a hearing. That was a good sign. If the judge granted the motion, he would be released directly from the courthouse to—but that was it, to where? To an in-patient drug treatment facility pending trial, most likely. Well, he reasoned, maybe it would be the first step down a long road leading away from what he was now.

He pictured his mother and father at the hearing, and felt a tug of emotion as he saw them reacting with pride as he agreed—no, *requested*—to go to Truth House. The old man would surely be pleased. It would be the start of a new relationship. Everything would be different.

He stood propped against the wall, trying to snuggle his other foot into the remaining shoe, when he heard the familiar voice.

"Brought you some breakfast, mister man," said Eugene Bowe, a thin smile curling his lips.

"What are you doin' here?" said Spaulding idiotically, as if they were in some prison movie.

"Jus' be on detail, helping Aikens get the solitaries fed," said Bowe. "Don't worry, I ain't gonna hurt you."

Spaulding felt the hot tingle of panic in his chest but fought the reaction, thinking it inappropriate. After all, the cell door was wide open and Aikens was just down the hallway, crooning some Delta song as he rattled Youngblood's door.

Bowe placed a breakfast tray carefully on the chair, then returned to the door.

"Heard you taught my man Proctor a few things the other day," he offered.

"Nah," said Spaulding, "wasn't nothin' really."

"You the man now. See you back the dorm," said Bowe, as he edged into the hallway.

Spaulding sat before his food, amazed at his good fortune. He was about to dig in to his chipped beef when Bowe loped back into the room, muttering "forgot something, Boss" in an apologetic tone. He moved as if toward Spaulding's tray, holding packets of condiments in his hands. Suddenly he threw the packets to the floor and in one swift movement placed his hands around Spaulding's arms, yanked him out of his chair and punched him full force on the side of the head.

"That's what you get for messin' with Proctor," he hissed.

Seconds later Bowe was in the hallway again, wheeling the food cart to the next cell as if nothing had happened.

Spaulding fell to the floor where he lay writhing, trying to lift a hand to his head. Eventually he succeeded, and began exploring the side of his skull with his fingers. His injured mind was suddenly certain that if he found the right spot and pressed hard against it, he could turn off the hurt and stop the leakage. He tried his best to find the spot, but couldn't. Gradually the pain increased and everything grew dim. He was surprised to see in the dimness that his father and a small child had appeared before him. He watched as his father pointed to a spot on the side of his injured head. The child then placed its hand on the spot, stroked it gently, and to Spaulding's great relief the pain disappeared. His impulse was to rise and embrace the two visitors, but his attention was drawn instead to the dark whirling shapes that led him to the black well of unconsciousness.

* * *

The next thing he knew he was nestled at the bottom of a snowdrift, gradually coming out of a deep sleep. He was lying flat, cocooned, protected by a wall of fluffy white snow. But protected from what? He didn't have a clue. Was he hiding? Buried? Should he dig his way through the drift and signal for help? He tried to move his legs but couldn't. He tried to focus his mind but couldn't. He drifted back to sleep.

Seconds later he was back in the snowdrift again, struggling up a high white tunnel toward the sound of voices. Above ground, people were talking about him in low, measured tones. Who were they? Friends or foes? He listened as best he could but couldn't follow their conversation—there was too much snow between him and them. He began to slip off yet again—part of him still yearned to embrace the familiar spinning darkness. But this time he forced himself to remain semi-conscious and continue climbing, in an effort to break through the drift and confront whatever awaited above.

A moment later his eyes fluttered open, revealing a metal bed painted brown, white sheets, a railing at the foot of the bed, and a cart with stainless steel implements on it. The smell of antiseptic pulled it all together for him: he was in the jail infirmary. The voices were those of medics discussing his condition.

He decided to feign sleep while he figured out how he'd arrived in the ward. He got only so far, then his head began to hurt and he had to let his thoughts go. They drifted along, in the backwaters of his mind, until he saw the Holton Arms on a shoreline and in an instant the past caught up with him: Latisha, the police, jail. Bowe. He had been about to leave for court . . . Bowe had come at him . . . that was all he could remember.

One of the orderlies asked him if he was awake.

"I'm gettin' there," he said. "But how'd I get here?"

The orderlies explained that Bowe's roundhouse to the head had given him a major concussion. Good thing he was such a hardhead, they chuckled, and told him he'd been out cold for two days.

"You'll get headaches for a while after the meds wear off but over the next few weeks you'll get better."

"Where is Eugene Bowe?" he asked.

"Solitary," came the reply, "Waiting for his trial. Don't worry, knuckle-head. He won't get anywhere near you."

They told him he would go to court on the bond review motion when he was better. They also told him his parents had sent him a letter, and that his lawyer had called.

He tried to think of the lawyer's name: Ms. Rosen . . . berg? . . . stein? . . . sweig? Rosenberg.

As he thought over the news from the orderlies, he realized his body felt different—not his head, which was bandaged and beginning to throb, but the rest of him. Some things were missing: the tingling sensation, the familiar pulsing of his muscles. They were gone. He felt calm and relaxed, as if he were waking up refreshed after a long afternoon nap. No purple dots spinning behind the—*what*—yes! It was the craving!—there was none! He was, just possibly, drug free for the first time in months, except for whatever they'd shot him up with to relieve the pain. He closed his eyes, digested the thought, and then let his mind wander as it wished. After a moment he saw himself soaring through the air, flying at treetop height over a forest of emerald green trees, growing from the roof of the Holton Arms. He smiled, realizing the vision was the work of his imagination, not the work of controlled substances, and went along for the ride.

* * *

As he rode the bouncing blue jail bus to the courthouse a week later, he remembered for the first time the moment when Bowe had hit him. He was lucky to be alive, and now he felt almost healthy. Plus his lawyer was on the case and his parents actually wanted him home again—or at least in treatment, near their house in D.C. Next he remembered his conversation with his father about Truth House, and the vision of the pool-playing youngster. His phantom child.

"Don't worry kid, I'm gonna make it," he said quietly, and this time no voice from within rose up in protest.

He looked through the bus window and saw back from the road a row of sugar maples standing in the mists of dawn. It was early spring and the buds on their bare limbs had not yet begun to turn into leaves. But he knew they had survived the winter: they had lived through a dark, fearsome time and now it was their time to grow. The thought made him smile.

The Four F's

In mid-January, as the ground crusted over and five inches of D.C. snow hinted at worse weather to come, Alonzo Davis and Maisha Dawkins drove the city's unplowed roads toward the 900 block of 12th Street, N.E.

"Got to get the wipers fixed on this car," said Davis. "Flakes are gigantic today."

"I'd focus on the heater, I was you," said Dawkins. "Maybe we should do this tomorrow."

"Tomorrow's booked. Court in the morning, then the jail. And I have motions to work on. Anyway people are more likely to be home on a Sunday."

"How's Grant holding up at the jail? Anyone messing with him?"

"He wouldn't tell me if they were. I told him if he got threats or anything to ask to be put in admin seg."

"You mean solitary."

"For his own safety. Can't believe Heartless Hartman denied our bond review motion."

As Davis pulled the car over to the curb near the end of the 800 block of 12th Street, Maisha pulled a blue nylon jacket out of her knapsack. On its back were the words "Washington Gas & Electric," written in large yellow letters. "I thought I'd wear this and carry a clipboard, so it would look like I'm going door to door to read meters or do a customer service survey."

"Maisha" Davis said, "that is a great idea. But when you talk to people, you can't say you're from Washington Gas. You need to say you're an investigator working for attorney Alonzo Davis and that he's representing someone who's the defendant in a court case. If they ask, a court case involving the shooting that happened in October. Can't mislead a potential witness, OK?"

"Got it. Don't let me freeze to death out there, 'Lonzo."

"I'll just stay a few houses behind you, so people don't think you're working with an undercover. That won't help."

"You right," Maisha replied. "Save me some coffee, cause I bet no one will talk to me. I mean, if the police say no one on the block said they knew anything, I just don't see why—"

"Because no one in this neighborhood wants to be seen talking to cops, period."

"I still have subpoenas to serve in the Freeman case."

"I know. I appreciate everything you're doing."

"This is getting old, and I have finals in two weeks."

"Maisha. You still want to be a criminal lawyer?"

"Save me the speech." Maisha opened the car's door and planted a booted foot into the snow bank by the curb. "See you soon, long as nobody shoots me."

"Be safe. I'll wait here unless someone invites you in. Then signal me and I'll be right there."

"Got it." Maisha slammed the door shut, crossed I Street N.E., and walked up to the first row house on the 900 block of 12th Street. She swore as she trudged through the snowdrift covering its walkway. The temperature had dipped to the low twenties, so she'd worn a sweatshirt and a sweater under her Washington Gas jacket, but the wind made her eyes water.

She walked up the steps to the house and knocked on its

front door. No answer. She waited, and then knocked again, louder and longer. No sign of activity within.

"One down," she said. She walked back to the sidewalk, gave Davis a thumbs down, and pushed on to the next house. She rang and knocked, with the same result.

As she made her way down the block, a few people invited her into the vestibules of their row houses after assuring themselves she wasn't a crime threat, a Jehovah's Witness or a magazine salesperson. But when she told them what she was searching for, they shook their heads and said they couldn't help her. Just as they'd told "that white detective," they were at work the day of the shooting, or out of town, or anywhere else they could think of besides home. It seemed the only thing they knew for sure was they knew nothing.

By the time she got to the row house at 943 12th Street N.E., three quarters of the way down the block, Maisha figured it was a lost cause. She pushed the doorbell, but it didn't ring. She knocked, but no one came to the door. It wasn't getting any warmer, and she thought how comfortable she could be next to the heater in Davis's Mustang, now parked by the curb a few houses up the street. She turned, walked down the stoop steps and made her way along the sidewalk toward the car.

When she got there, Davis rolled the window down. "What's up?"

"Doorbell's not working. Plus I need to warm up a while before I go to the next house—if I go to a next house."

"Mi, if we're gonna do this, let's do it right. That doorbell must have been out of whack when the cops made their way down the block, and like you they were probably ready to head home by the time they got to it—so when the bell didn't work, they packed it in. Which you shouldn't do, because this house is almost directly across the street from the yard the victim was running for. Actually slightly farther down the street from the yard—which makes for a better view of the scene than that offered by the house across from it. Better angle of vision to see the hit. So how about you down a cup of coffee," he said, reaching for his thermos, "and then take a second pass at that house."

Maisha frowned and shook her head. She didn't like hearing Davis's lecture. The guy had repeatedly told her it was necessary to investigate the heck out of these cases to do the job right and give their clients a fighting chance. Davis called it the Four F's: Find the Friggin' Facts Fast. And he didn't always use the word Friggin'.

"It's freezing and no one's answering." Maisha put the thermos down and rubbed her hands together in front of the heater vent. "Maybe we should come back another day."

"Mi. You know the drill. We have to follow down every lead if we want to do the job right—and defend—*really* defend—clients like Tony Grant. He says he didn't do it. And if you're planning to be a defense attorney, this is key. Great criminal lawyers are investigation fanatics. That's why I say—"

"I know, the Four F's."

"Find the Friggin' Facts Fast. Look. Choosing not to—"

"I know. 'Choosing not to track down every lead is choosing to lose the case.'"

"Well put. Who was it said that?"

"You did, as you well know. Or maybe it was Clarence Darrow."

"Could have been Earl Rogers. How 'bout Johnnie Cochran?"

"Don't worry, I'll give the house a second try. First I need to defrost."

They sat in the Mustang in silence. Maisha opened the thermos and poured herself a cup of coffee.

"This coffee's really strong, you should try mixing it with water."

"Just leave me half a cup."

Maisha gulped down her coffee and handed the thermos and cup to Davis. "They shoot me, you get the rest."

"You should be OK. Eighth and H Street territory is blocks away.

"That's reassuring."

"Just kidding. They're long gone."

Maisha pushed the Mustang's door open and walked back to the ramshackle house numbered 943 and knocked on the door again. There was no response. She watched a few more snowflakes trickle to the ground, tried the bell again and knocked some more. Then she called out, "Gas company, here to make sure you've got heat for the winter!"

Still nothing. She cursed and jammed her hands into her jacket pockets to warm them. She looked at the Mustang, shrugged, and made her way back down the slippery steps, but couldn't help looking over her shoulder at the house one more time as she edged down the walkway. When she did, she saw a face in the third floor window. She waved before she could think about it and the person in the window, who looked to be an old man, waved back. Maisha turned and showed the man the back of her jacket. The man held his index finger up as if to say, wait a minute.

"No problem, I'm waiting," Maisha called out. "Probably shoot me when he finds out I'm not the gas man." She tightened her scarf and turned and looked back at the

Mustang and gave Davis a thumbs up to let him know what was going on.

After what seemed an eternity the front door opened, revealing an elderly man supporting himself with a cane and a hand firmly grasping the doorway's painted-over woodwork.

"I wonder can you give me a hand with my space heater, Miss? It don't seem to work no more. Had it for years and it's put out heat jus' fine, but for some reason it's on the blink now."

"I'll be happy to ah, take a look at it. You mind if I ask my friend in the car over there to come in with me?"

"Long as he's with the gas company."

Maisha turned toward the street, signaled Davis to wait, stomped the snow off her boots and entered the vestibule. She said, "I'll talk to him later," and followed the man up the stairway.

"They got apartments on every floor, but the second floor's empty," the man said as they climbed the stairs. It took several minutes for them to reach the third floor. The man was unsteady on his feet and his cane was of little use to him on the steps. Once they were inside the apartment, the man introduced himself as Benjamin Harris and showed Maisha the space heater. It was plugged in and turned on, but as Harris said, not putting out any heat.

Maisha knelt beside the heater, which looked old enough to be the first such device off the assembly line. She moved the dial around. On, off, on, nothing. She looked over the frayed black and white wire leading to a socket a few feet away and stood up.

"I think it's pretty much broken, Mr. Harris. I mean like beyond repair."

As soon as she said that the heater began making crinkly noises and as they watched, its coils turned pink and then bright red.

"Damn, you good luck, young lady. I been tryin' to make that happen for days."

"Timing is everything," said Maisha, but no sooner had she spoken than the device sputtered, sent a few sparks flying, and cut off again.

"I'll tell you what, Mr. Harris. That thing isn't working right, and when it's on, it's dangerous. It could go on by itself in the night, or when you're out somewhere, and look—it's only a few feet from these curtains. They could go up in flames in seconds and start a major fire."

"I need those curtains there too, help keep the place warm."

"Tell you what I'll do. You got this thing because the landlord's not heating the house, right?"

"That's exac'ly right. Landlord, he ain't done a thing but collect the rent for years. Does that pretty good. He don't turn the heat on til December the fifteenth and even when it's on the building's still cold—like now."

"You give me his name, and I'll see what I can do."

"Now hold on a minute. I don't want him thinking I complained about him or nothing. I live alone now and I'm too old to go lookin' for a new place to live. Got a lot of snow on my roof," he added, running his hand across the white hair on his head. "I'm not fixin' to wind up on the street. I mean I got my sister and all but . . . ."

"He won't know it was you. I'll check some records downtown and have someone from the city look into it. We'll get you some heat. But promise me you won't use that heater, it's dangerous."

"Huh. Hasn't burned the place down yet." He looked out his bay window to the street. "They oughta burn this whole block down anyway; there's nothin' but criminals out there. You see that house across the street?"

"With the low brick wall?"

"That very one. A couple months back I'm lookin' out the window here minding my own business, and up pulls this truck stops right in the middle the block and some young man in a camouflaged jacket gets out and shoots a man walking across the street. He was runnin' actually, the man what got shot, trying to make it to the tall grass in the yard I 'spect when they shot him. Can you imagine? Right in the middle of broad daylight. At first I thought OK, it's a government secret service thing, with the shiny new truck and the camouflaged and all. I figured it was some kinda official business. Undercovers or something. But it weren't; the man did the shooting had on blue jeans, no kind a uniform at all—and those locks, what do they call them—"

"Dreadlocks?"

"Yeah, that stick out ever which way from they head, look like they're from another planet with TV antennas comin' out they brain, I swear to God. Anyway he went on across the street and shot the poor man again and then he went and got a—what do you call—oh yeah, a tarp and covered the man up with it. After that he run back to the truck and they jus' drove away—slow, like nothin' much had happened."

"Then what?"

Harris shrugged. "Whole neighborhood's like that, it's got so's I don't want to go out unless to shop. Do that in the daylight cause slow as I walk, those street boys be on me in a flash."

"Listen I want to ask you some questions about that shooting."

"Like to of scared the pants off me, it did."

"Did you get a good look at the person who shot the man?"

"I'd say pretty good. He was tall. Big, like he'd played football or some other sports. Looked to be in his twenties, youngish. Had a gun with a long barrel—I can tell you what they were driving though. It was one a them small-size Ford trucks, a green F-150. Looked to be a almos' brand new one, or maybe a year old model. F-150s, they call 'em."

"The shooter got out of a truck? He wasn't walking down the street? Are you sure about that?"

"I sure am. And I know my cars and trucks, Miss. See cause my grandson stay here from time to time, and he's eleven and plumb crazy about 'em. Makes me look at all the pictures in this book he has. I even watch the car commercials now, so I can tell him about prices and the mile per gallon. He's a good kid. One time when he—"

"Let me tell you something before you tell me anything else. I have another job that's more important than any Washington Gas gig."

"All right, but if you don't mind I need to sit down. These knees a mine is shot."

Harris lowered himself carefully onto a plain, straight-backed wooden chair. Maisha was relieved to see the chair had a flat seat and a sturdy back.

"I called nine one eleven when I seen it all, and they sent the police right away."

"Did you give them your name when you called?"

"No, I . . . I can't say I did. When you get to be my age, you don't want to get involved in things like that. I figure I reported it and that proved to be, ah, what's the word . . .

sufficient enough to get the police out here. Not that they ever arrest anyone an' if they do, they're back on the street the next day seems like."

"Listen, I'm actually a law student at Georgetown Law School, working part-time on a case. Here, you can take a look at this card."

Harris read the card, nodded, and smiled.

"Gonna be a lawyer, huh? Amazes me, how they got so many black lawyers now. An' they sure need 'em, the crime we got to put up with."

"I hear you. So listen, I'm working with an attorney on a case related to the shooting you saw. We're representing the person who's been charged with the offense."

"Oh. I didn't realize that. I'm not sure I want to get dragged into all that. That's why I didn't give my name when I called it in."

"The thing is, our client's been charged, but he has no record and says he didn't do the crime. Based on what we know, we don't think he did either."

Harris nodded. "Sometimes they arrest the wrong one. You're not going to make me go to court, are you?"

"That's not up to me. You don't even have to talk with us if you don't want to."

"I'm not lookin' to get nobody out there angry at me, you know."

"Our client's in jail and he's pretty angry about that. Plus if he's innocent, that means the real shooter is still out there."

Harris nodded again and scratched the snow-white hair on his head.

"I work with an attorney at the D.C. Public Defender Service. Basically we represent people charged with a crime who have no money. People who can't afford to hire a lawyer to defend them."

"Well I guess I'll talk with you. Already done told you most of what I saw."

"OK if I tell my attorney to join us?"

"All right then. Where is he?"

"He's in a car a few houses down the block. If you want I can go get him."

"How's about I just wave him in from the window, like I did with you?"

"That would be great." Maisha watched as Harris went to his bay window and lifted the sash.

"What kind a car?" asked Harris.

"It's a blue Mustang, about ten years old."

"I got it. Mustang's one of his favorite cars. My grandson, I mean."

Harris stuck his hand out the window and waved. "He seen me; he's getting out the car. Lot of snow out there for December, we could be in for a long winter." He shut the window and sat back down in the chair. "You can sit too, you know. On the sofa over there. Don't mind the plastic covering, it's squeaky but it keeps the sofa clean. I don't do much cleaning these days since my wife done passed, so...."

"I understand." Maisha sat and took a pen and a legal pad out of her knapsack. "Please read over the card carefully ... I want to be sure you understand I'm investigating the shooting you saw, for an attorney who's involved in the case."

"Sorry it's not warmer in here. You want a cup of coffee, or maybe some tea?"

"No, thanks. I'm fine."

They sat in silence for a moment, then Maisha said, "OK if I go downstairs and let him in?"

"I'd appreciate not havin' to climb those stairs again."

Maisha told Harris she'd be right back, and headed for the stairs, trying to contain her excitement. At the front door, she motioned Davis inside. Moments later, as Davis stomped the snow off his boots, she told him "This guy's the caller. He gave me a description of the shooter and the car they used. It doesn't fit our guy!"

"Let's see if we can get a written statement from him."

"I've got my pad out already."

"Maisha."

"This is great. What?"

"This is why we do this stuff. Neither rain nor snow—"

"I know, the Four F's."

"I'm telling you."

"I hear you."

"Let's go!"

They raced up the steps, toward the third floor of the house.

A Shooting on R Street

Ward Simmons waited as Rucker leaned forward and put his orange-clad elbows on the D.C. Jail's shiny steel tabletop. If Rucker was as flush as he claimed, the hit would bring in at least five grand. Maybe six.

"Sim. When they bought me up to court for the arrangement—"

"Arr*aign*ment."

"Whatever. My lawyer say a person who live on the block saw the shooting and he gonna testify for the government."

"You got a name? Look Ruck, my head's throbbing and I didn't get much rack time last night."

"Lawyer say he don't know. Jus it's a old man use a walkin' stick to get around with."

Simmons paused for effect before popping the question. "So, you need me to help you out with this problem?"

"Yeah, I do. I know I messed up, catchin' this beef. You gonna stick with me, man?"

"I'm with you, Ruck. You're our main man in D.C. and sales are up. Way up. So this bump in the road—we make it go away. Course your guys shot that kid on your say-so, and you should never have done that. Now you're in here, now there's this prosecution. All these complications. Which means you're gonna have to pay for Special Ed and Company's services."

"Solid. I 'preciate that."

"Cost you six grand though."

"Huh?" Rucker made a face like someone had stepped on his foot. "What about three gran'?"

"Going rate now is six to do that kind of job. You been in the joint over a month now, and meanwhile prices gone up." Simmons shrugged. "Too much heat on the street, man."

"Look, I can't get to all my cash while I'm in here. But I'm good for three gran'. I'll get Carson to front it."

"Ruck. You know the reason Special Ed keeps three shooters on payroll? Two other than me?"

"He got a business to run?"

"Case one of us gets uppity, the others keep him in line. People in this business tend to forget who they work for. 'Who calls the shots,' I think the expression is. But Ed don't tolerate that, he never did. And either do I . . . . We clear?"

Rucker sighed and fingered the bruise on his arm. "We clear, but I ain't being uppity. Come on, what about three gran'?"

"You know Ruck . . . think about how am I going to find this witness, I ain't got a name? Old man with a walking' stick. Huh. This'll be a tough job."

"It's only a block, Sim. Sixteen hundred block, Lincoln Road, right off North Cap."

"Which is dead center, R Street crew territory. And you know what those dudes do."

"I know. It's rough over there, you ain't lying."

"It's more than rough. R Street crew is mowing people down. What I hear, you're not running with them, they'll shoot you just for making it some other way. Lincoln and R's a shooting gallery after dark."

"Then jus'—you know, have one of your boys hang there until they spot the dude. Then it's a quick in an' out."

"One a my boys—huh. Ward Simmons ain't got no boys. Sim's the name and solo's my game, least when it comes to witnesses. Too many cooks, man. You know how I got my scar?" he asked, fingering the lily-white line on the left side of his neck.

Rucker nodded. "You done tole me like three times."

"Quarter inch to the right and I'd a been DOA at Saint Agnes. So no disrespect, but I'll have to take a look around there myself. If I can't find the man before—wait."

Simmons glanced over at the sullen turnkey who was eyeing them, and put his finger to his lips to signal Rucker to lower his voice. Then he turned and glared at the guard until the man turned his head and moved away from them, toward the cellblock door.

"Takes care a him. So if I can't find the wit, it may not be til the first day of the trial that I do him. I'll see the cops pick him up and take him to court that morning. They always do that day one, make sure their wits show. Then I'll know where he lives. And after they bring him back there at the end the day, and they're gone, he's gone."

"Sound like a plan, but—"

"A six grand plan. Cause if you want to hang on to this business—which is making you a rich man, am I right?"

"Gettin' there."

"So I'm saying, you're gonna stay in the game, then you need to get your ass out of this place soon as you can. Otherwise things have a way of happening. You know, people start thinking it's their turn 'cause you're in here, sidelined. And before we know it, certain things take their course."

Simmons fingered his scar and stared at Rucker and waited. Rucker cracked his knuckles but said nothing.

"OK. For you, Ruck: five grand. But don't tell no one."

"Yeah. Thanks Sim, you on. Five grand. I'll talk to Carson."

"Excellent. You get me the cash; I'm on it in a flash. I'm gonna lighten your load, man. Get to turn that orange-aid jumpsuit in and go home."

"Solid. I'll get Carson run it over to Special Ed."

"That'll do." Simmons stood. "I'll be in touch, Ruck. Hang tight for now—you're gonna walk."

They shook hands and Simmons signaled the guard to escort him back to the main visitors' section of the jail.

* * *

Shortly after sunrise the following Friday, Simmons sat slumped down in a maroon mini-van, watching a heavy-set uniformed officer walk up the steps to 1629 Lincoln and ring the bell. He was still fighting a bad cold—maybe it was another bout of the flu—and was feeling weak and drowsy. The humid mid-summer heat didn't help. But the rollers were true to form, and now he had the address of the eyewitness in Rucker's murder case.

He'd planned everything down to the last detail, as always. He'd borrowed the early eighties van he sat in from Special Ed, because unlike his '91 Mercedes it was sure to blend in with the other heaps on the block. But it turned out the rollers didn't even scout the block. He could have been driving a Rolls and they wouldn't have noticed. The rollers. Simmons remembered the blacks in his neighborhood calling the officers jump-outs when he was a kid because they "jumped out" of their cruiser as soon as they pulled up, and chased down whoever they were after. By the time he got out of the Marines, the bloods were calling them rollers, so he did too. The lingo changed fast.

The roller driving the cruiser kept his eyes on the fat one, who was now knocking on the door of the row house, so Simmons knew he didn't have to worry about being caught rubbernecking as he wrote the address down on a liquor store paper bag. Even if they saw him, he knew he wouldn't stand out. He'd made every effort to pass as an ordinary guy. Covered the flaming dice tattoo on his arm, wore his red hair short, parted on the side and neatly trimmed. Topped it off with a well-ironed button-down shirt. Some gangstas mocked the way he dressed for work, but he felt they were dumb. His mantra was, "If you want a head start, don't dress the part."

The fat roller knocked again—longer this time. Seconds later a light went on in the building's third-story window, and someone poked his head out between the curtains and waved to the officer. The old man, he thought. So he'd lived his life anyway—he just didn't know it yet. That was probably the window he'd seen the shooting go down from.

Simmons reviewed his plan while he waited for the officer to fetch the witness. Now that he knew where the old man lived, he would do him this evening, after midnight when there wasn't much activity on the street. But what would he do in the meantime? He thought immediately of Janice, an old flame—actually, more than a flame—who lived minutes away in Shaw. She'd supposedly kicked her drug habit, and would be a sure-fire roll in the sack. He wanted her, badly. But she was special and something told him not to call her. He told himself he didn't want to pass his flu on to her. Besides, he needed to be fully alert when kill time came. Maybe the thing to do was scoot back home to Charm City—on the way, make a quick stop to score one of the beauties at the pay-by-the-hour motel out New York Avenue—and then nap off until the evening.

A couple of minutes later, the front door to the row house opened and the old man stood stooped and thin in the doorframe. The roller shook hands with him and helped him down the steps. He scoped the street once, left to right, but Simmons saw it was a cursory look, taken more from habit than caution, and wrote the roller off as a threat.

They had trouble getting their witness into the back seat of the cruiser. Too much bending for old bones. But soon they had him strapped in the shotgun seat. The driver gunned the engine and the cruiser knifed into the street, picking up speed as it passed the van.

Simmons smiled. They were gone. On their way to North Capitol Street and then southbound, to the courthouse.

He waited a long time before easing out of the van and crossing the street. The sun had barely risen, but he felt its heat on his back as he walked toward the old man's building. It promised to be a scalding hot day, and he was already sweating from every pore. He stood in front of the house for several minutes before moving partway up the walkway to the steps. From that close-in vantage point he gauged the strength of the front door and took in the style and brand of the security lock. After that he cut across the building's meager front yard and trotted along its north side to the alleyway that ran behind it. If there was a second-story window in the back wall of the structure, he could pry it open and get to the staircase come nightfall. That would be a snap.

But there was no such window—only a solid brick wall. He pawed the gravel in the alley with one of his spit-shined Tony Lama boots while he considered his options. He'd just have to wait until dark and go in through the front door. Meanwhile he'd head back to Baltimore and get some rest.

* * *

That evening, Simmons returned to the 1600 block of Lincoln Road N.E. and scoped out the old man's building as he rolled by in Special's minivan. His Rolex now glowed ten-fifteen. The rollers would have brought the old man back from court in the afternoon, so now it was time to execute the plan. And the man, he thought, smiling. He was so sharp—no wonder the femmes loved him.

He took his Beretta out of the glove compartment and checked it out again. Fully loaded. Nice looking piece. He dug hearing the sharp metallic click that sounded when he took the safety off. He clicked it off and on for a bit and finally put it back on and told himself to be patient. Go over the plan again in his head.

The target building's third-floor lights were out, so he figured the old guy was sleeping and he would have to make his way in and up the stairs in the dark. Trouble was, there was still too much activity on the street for him to make his move. He considered visiting Janice, just to say hello and chat, and returning to the block afterward. But no, he had too much to do tonight. Plus the jury was still out on whether the night sweats he'd had in the spring were from something worse than the flu—and if so, he didn't want to pass that something on to Janice. He was probably OK, but if he saw her one thing could lead to another and why take the chance.

He needed to check out the neighborhood, so he took a long slow look around the 1600 block, and then drove over to Quincy, which ran east to west one block north of Lincoln. No one was out on the street or hanging on the front steps of the row houses: the block looked closed for business. He figured it would remain that way until after midnight, when things would pick up again. Deals would be transacted in the alleys; scores would be settled in the shadows. He'd take care of his own business in the meantime.

He drove back to North Capitol and double-parked a few blocks from Lincoln, figuring he'd cool his jets until eleven p.m. At that hour it would be pitch dark, and Lincoln Road would be silent.

He glanced at the week's worth of mail he'd thrown into the van's back seat before driving back to the District, and decided to paw through it while he waited. A white business envelope among the circulars caught his eye. It was from the clinic. He stared at it, wondering if he should just throw it out the window and live with the uncertainty. Then he said "fuck it" and ripped it open. A few seconds later he had his answer: Dear Mr. Simmons, etc. . . . had tested positive for HIV and was strongly advised to return to the clinic to begin treatment immediately.

So his suspicion had been correct—the February Flu From Hell had been an early indicator, and whatever he was suffering from now meant he was on his way to the AIDS ward. The realization took his breath away. He'd been living a kill for cash life for the past few years and good as he was, had figured sooner or later either the cops or a gang-banger from Rayful's crew would blow him away. But this? What was the "treatment" for this shit, really? He knew there was no cure; it wasn't called the Death Virus for nothing. You thinned out, chunks of your body turned purple, people ignored you and you died. There was no cure. They'd figured out a way to prolong the agony, some non-stop, expensive set of drugs. But at some point his people would find out and think he was a fruit. Special Ed would shoot him soon as he heard, figuring he was contagious and bad for business. Damn it all!

He sat in the van, recycling these thoughts and chain-smoking his Pall Malls. He remembered the grunt from Desert Storm advising him, the night before he bled out, "You can ride horses bareback, but not the ladies." At the time, the kid probably meant VD, the Syph. But really, AIDS? AIDS was something gay people got. He knew two guys who'd caught it, and hadn't visited them once he heard the news. Hadn't spent all that much time thinking about them, either. Same with drug addicts who used infected needles. He lived by a strict code and it was simply a matter of "you engage in that behavior, you deserve what you get." But now he found himself thinking about their plight—and how on earth they coped with it—for close to an hour. Now, he had something in common with them.

He considered bagging the job—in his current condition, it made more sense to just drive home, have a few drinks and hit the crib. Sleep it off; deal with it in the morning. But if he whiffed and the witness testified, Rucker or Special—especially Special—might decide ol' Sim was expendable. Yeah. Anyway, the old man would be an easy mark, and the five grand might pay for a month or two of whatever they pumped into him to keep him in pre-AIDS status. Who knows, maybe he could keep it a secret and there'd be a cure down the line. Probably too far down the line, though.

He decided he'd better do the job. Hot as it was, between the heat and his night sweats, he donned gloves and a hoodie before he got out of Special Ed's van. He walked around the corner to Lincoln, which was still quiet except for the occasional car heading south, toward North Capitol. He pulled the hoodie tighter to make his pale face less noticeable in the neighborhood and walked slowly down the street to number 1629. He quick-stepped up the walkway to the front steps. There he checked out the street again. No one on foot—that made sense given the nature of the neighborhood. No cars coming down the block now. He took a small iron bar out of his hoodie pouch and wedged it between the door and its frame, just above the lock, and pushed on the bar to pull the frame toward him. The sound of the traffic on North Capitol muffled the snap and splintering of the wood. Soon there was enough space between the door and the frame for him to reach behind the door and grasp the knob used to lock it by extending a bolt of steel into the frame. He turned the knob and watched the bolt retract until it was flush with the edge of the door. That left only the silver chain connecting the door to the latch on the frame. It hung before him at eye level, glistening in the star-filled summer night.

An image of a headstone appeared in his mind for a second but he shook it off. Refocused. Pulled a small pair of bolt cutters out of his pocket and snipped both sides of a link in the chain. The link broke into two pieces, dangling impotently from their fixtures. His pathway cleared, he turned once more to the street and scanned the block. Seeing no activity, he eased the door open, slipped into the foyer and closed the door behind him.

The staircase before him was barely revealed by a lone low-watt light bulb hanging from the ceiling. He took the stairs two at a time and made the third floor in about thirty seconds. Took a moment to catch his breath before he walked down the hallway to the apartment door. The lock on the door looked as flimsy as the one on the street door, but instead of forcing it he knocked gently on the unstained wood and waited.

No response. He knocked harder. Nothing. No sense of movement inside. Could it be the old guy wasn't home? That didn't make any sense. More likely he was asleep. And if he was sleeping so soundly he didn't hear the knocking, he wouldn't hear the lock being forced.

Mother-fucking AIDS! No, HIV. Not yet AIDS. Ok, just— block it out and finish the job.

Using the same tools, he disengaged the lock, opened the door, and entered the apartment. He waited a full two minutes by the door while his eyes adjusted to the darkness. Then he glided silently down the hallway. He'd worn old U.S. Keds he knew wouldn't squeak, just in case he had to sneak through the apartment this way. A few more steps to the living room. Empty. TV off, space heater off, low-level light from a nearby streetlamp entering from the front windows. No brighter than the light made by a fading flashlight battery. He turned and tiptoed past the tiny kitchen to the back hallway. He opened the bathroom door, inch by inch, just to be safe. It was empty. Smelled like Clorox. A few more steps and he stood before what had to be the bedroom door. He stood stock still before the door for three long minutes, timing himself on his Rolex. Not a sound from within. No sounds elsewhere in the house either, or from the street. "Not a creature was stirring, not even a mouse." The line ran through his head. It was time.

He pulled the Beretta out of his left blue jean pocket. It felt snug in his hand—small and light. He pushed the safety off, cocked the weapon, opened the door and stepped into the bedroom, ready to fire.

The bed was empty. He saw the closet door was half open so he strode over to it and pushed it open the rest of the way with his foot. The closet was also empty. He bent over and looked under the bed. A trunk, a couple of boxes, dust. But no one cowering on the floor.

"You old-ass sonofabitch," he said quietly. "Where the hell are you?"

Had he made a mistake? Was this the wrong night? No, he was on the money, but somehow the old man was gone. He stood still a moment, pondering his next move, before walking back to the apartment door. He peeked through the space he'd made forcing it open, but saw nothing in the dim light other than the empty staircase. It was time to book. He tiptoed down the stairs, opened the front door with care, then bolted down the stoop steps to the street, muttering "motherfucker" repeatedly under his breath. He pocketed the pistol and tightened the hoodie around his face as he ran to the corner of Quincy and North Capitol Street, heading back to the van.

As he made his way down the sidewalk on the north side of Quincy, he saw a young man walking toward him, head down—a kid, really—wearing jeans and a U.S. Army field jacket. He quickened his step as he approached the kid. The youngster didn't give ground so Simmons hissed "out of my way, punk" and shoved his left shoulder into him, hard, as he moved by him. The kid muttered "scumbag" under his breath as he recovered his footing and continued on his way.

Simmons spun around, pulled out his Beretta and let the kid walk another few steps before pointing it squarely at his back. Then he hesitated, took a deep breath, lowered the gun and let the kid walk on. After all he was in R Street territory and it would not be wise to attract attention. The sharp crack of the gunshot would echo in the warm night air. And, the kid might be connected.

He watched as the kid made his way down the block and disappeared into the night. He felt good about giving the kid a break. Letting someone live for a change, doing something good in the world before he—right, right. He took a deep breath, coughed, caught his breath and decided. What a night! It was the first job he'd ever messed up, but so what, Rucker would go nuts and call Special Ed and they'd do to him exactly what he'd planned to do to the old man. What goes around comes around: as of tonight he was toast, despite all his planning. Infected toast, actually.

He tried to think of a story he could make up, to convince them events prevented him from making the kill. But it was hard to concentrate, now that it seemed he was up against two possible death sentences.

He was a scumbag, no question, but at least he'd done a couple of good things along the way. Saved a few grunts during the war. Let the kid in the field jacket live, and best of all, had refrained from passing on his disease—Was that what it was? A disease?—to Janice. Janice and Ward, the one possible love affair of his life.

One way out would be to get the jump on them and use the Beretta on himself. He took a good long look at it. Admired its clean sliver lines before raising it to his temple. One bullet and he'd be gone, left in a heap for someone to shovel off the sidewalk. But his hand shook—he didn't have the nerve.

On the other hand, here he was, smack in the middle of R Street territory! That was the solution—it would be a matter of do unto others so they would do unto him. He walked a few yards north, toward the lone street light on the block. Standing under it, fully in its glow, he fired a shot at a nearby car window. The explosion echoed in the night, followed by the sound of shattered glass. Surely enough noise to attract attention.

"There will be no AIDS," he whispered.

He waited about a minute in the aftermath, but there was

no response, so he fired again. Three shots in rapid succession this time, loud enough to wake the dead.

"Who you think you are, Slim?" said a voice from somewhere in the darkness.

"I'm Ward Simmons and I say the hell with you and the hell with the R Street crew," he yelled.

The gunfire didn't begin immediately. He saw himself on the firing range at Quantico for a split second, saw the tracers streaming toward the targets but it was weird, the targets were all him, his face was on every stick. He was puzzling that out when *wham*, it began. It felt like he was being stung by hornets, a horde of hornets, lots and lots of them, bad, bad hornets with stingers like hammers. It was his last, brief thought as he sank to his knees, fell forward and hit the pavement face first.

The air around him soon smelled of cordite.

"Teach you to fuck with the crew," said the voice in the darkness, and once again the street was silent.

A Day in The Life

As the minutes ticked by in the empty courtroom, on a late August day of reckoning for her client, Annette James tried to gather her thoughts and cobble together her closing argument. Once the noon recess ended, it would be time for her to present Terrell Williams' defense. But if she had no witnesses—other than his girlfriend Keisha—she'd have to make her closing in less than an hour. She knew she would need a compelling closing to earn Terrell a not guilty verdict, yet she was unable to craft it, unable to weave the right words into place. Instead, she found herself wondering what had become of her investigator, Lester Settle.

She'd sent Lester across the river to Anacostia two days ago in a last-ditch effort to assess the credibility of Dawan Turner—Terrell's potential second witness. Annette had Dawan under subpoena, in the courthouse and ready to testify. She just wasn't sure he was telling the truth when he said his friend Terrell wasn't the shooter. He said he saw someone else, a blood wearing a red T-shirt, fire the shots. This information—if believed—would likely make Terrell's mistaken identification defense a winner. Lester's job was to check out the kid's story with his contacts on the street. If it held water, she'd put him on the stand.

There'd been no word from Lester for a full day, and it wasn't like him not to call or show up. She'd sent him into high crime areas time and again over the years, and he'd always managed to return unscathed, crucial witness or telltale documents in hand. Until recently, she'd tended not to worry about him, even when he was hoofing it on the far side of the Anacostia River. But D.C.'s body count for the year was on track to hit four hundred, and the betting was Anacostia would account for half that number all by itself. So while she did her best to picture Lester easing down alleyways and edging by the city's tense, spring-loaded cops as he ran down leads, it was hard not to be concerned.

Half an hour later, Annette and prosecutor Eleanor Flynn stood as the bailiff called out "all rise" and Judge John Lake entered the courtroom. As Lake eased his heavy frame down behind the mahogany bench, the victim, Earl Kubic, wheeled himself into the room. A white kid from the suburbs, Kubic had grown tired of smoking joints by the Seven-Eleven and run restless to the big-time city to score some coke. Things went third rail for him when it turned out he was short on the money. The rollers said Terrell had shot the kid four times, teaching him the ways of the street in one easy lesson. Now he sat in the back-room shadows, in the metal contraption he'd remain in until he healed.

A moment later, the chatter of hallway voices spilled into the room. Annette turned to see the cause of the commotion and was relieved to see Lester taking a seat in the spectator's section.

"Your Honor," she said, "On behalf of Mr. Williams, I would ask the court to extend the jury's luncheon recess by another twenty minutes. My investigator just arrived in the courtroom, and I need to discuss a—a very important matter with him before proceeding with the defense case." She glanced at Lester, who looked rumpled and unshaven, and was pleased to see his shoulder holster wasn't showing. "Your Honor knows Mr. Settle from—"

"Yes, I know Lester Settle, Miss James. Now with respect to your motion: we resumed this trial an hour later than usual this morning at your request, and here we are again, right after the lunch break, with yet another defense request for delay. If there's an objection, I'm inclined—Miss Flynn?"

"The government doesn't object to twenty minutes. It's a little late to be preparing the defense, but assault with intent to kill is a serious offense, and in the interest of justice …"

Annette bristled but bit her tongue. Eleanor Flynn was not her favorite Assistant U. S. Attorney, and her "it's late to be preparing the defense" comment was annoying. But bottom line, Flynn was fair. She had forgone an opportunity to gain an advantage over the defense by not opposing the request. The important thing now was to stay calm and get the recess.

"Your Honor," Annette said without inflection, "we're prepared, but something significant has just come up."

"The thing is, Miss James, you're asking me to delay the trial and inconvenience the jurors, for a reason you haven't even revealed to the court."

"What I can say is, it's a matter that may affect the outcome of the case. The rest is confidential, and as Your Honor knows, I can only discuss it with my client."

Lake frowned, stifled a response, and took a deep breath instead. He glanced at his watch and tapped a pencil on his bench top. Annette said nothing further, figuring his hesitation signaled he might cave.

"Very well," he said a moment later. "If such an issue has —indeed —surfaced, I have to—I'm obliged to give the defense time to work it out."

"Thank you, Your Honor."

Lake sighed, granted her fifteen minutes, and left for chambers.

Annette looked around the courtroom while the marshal handcuffed Terrell and walked him back to his holding cell. She took in the threadbare carpet in the well of the court, the zigzag scratches on the oak table before her, and the off-kilter slant of the empty chairs in the jury box. It seemed the furnishings in all the courtrooms of the Superior Court for the District of Columbia were either marred or worn down from years of nonstop use. She felt a bit frayed around the edges herself. Terrell's case was turning out to be more of a contest than she'd counted on.

In the days when she was a public defender, imagining the words "Equal Justice Under Law" were written on the barren back wall of a courtroom usually served to boost her adrenalin level in moments like this. Give her the strength she needed to fight through the roughest stretches of felony trials. After all, those four words—engraved on the portico above the entrance to the United States Supreme Court—articulated a goal it was her job to fight for whenever she defended an indigent client.

But she knew those words wouldn't deliver an emotional lift this time out, because Terrell was anything but indigent. In fact, he was six or seven figures beyond being a man without means. She was a solo practitioner with a great track record, and he'd paid her well, perhaps too well, to take on his case. But in return, he was expecting her to deliver something more than equal justice: he was expecting her to deliver an acquittal. So thinking lofty thoughts wasn't going to get her through the afternoon, and truth be told, the quality of the room's furnishings, like the leanings of the jurist handling her case, were irritants at most. What she needed to do was what she always did: stiffen her back, fulfill her professional obligation to her client, and give him the best defense she could muster.

After Terrell disappeared from view, she walked toward the back of the courtroom to greet Settle, who was wearing a frown and holding a printout in his hand. Kubic glared at her, fists clenched, as she walked by him. She figured he was still smarting from the cross-examination she'd subjected him to earlier in the day.

Right, that's what I did, took him apart as best I could, because guess what it's the adversary system, it's dog eat dog, survival of the fittest, she thought as she walked past Kubic.

Then she did a U-turn, walked back to him, leaned over and said, "Earl, I'm sorry about your injuries, I really am. I'm sorry for all of this."

Before he could react, she left him and made for the door, where Settle was now standing. Maybe she'd chickened out, but she wasn't sure she could handle what the kid might say in reply. Besides, the trial wasn't over, Judge Lake kept a stopwatch, and time was tight.

"Hey, Lester," she said in a low tone, as they shook hands and turned their backs to Flynn. "I was worried about you. Looks like you haven't slept much."

"No ma'am."

"No gun in the holster, right?"

"It's in the car—I had to dress for Southeast."

"Got it. Let's go to the hallway and talk. You find anything for me on Dawan?"

"Sure did," he said as they left the courtroom. "Take a look at the lockup list for May 25th. Number forty-two."

Annette scanned the list, leaned against the wall in the

dimly lit hallway, and shook her head. "If Dawan was in the lockup the morning of the 25th, then he was arrested the night of the 24th. He couldn't have seen the shooting, unless he was arrested after ten p.m."

"Which he wasn't: arrest record says the blood was wearing cuffs by six forty-five. And I verified that with the duty officer."

She'd been surprised when Terrell trotted his pal Dawan into her office a week before trial and told her he would testify the person who shot Kubic was wearing a red shirt. She knew Terrell wore a yellow shirt that night; he was wearing it in a party photo taken at his girlfriend Keisha's house. But she also knew Terrell carried a lot of weight in his neighborhood; not just his two hundred pounds of body fat but the kind of weight that made people jump when he called their name. So she'd told them both she wouldn't put on any false testimony, and then sent Lester to check out Dawan's story.

"Better to find out now than during Flynn's cross," said Lester. "Then again, she might not know about it."

"You think? Come on. She's in there salivating so much she might need a napkin. Pouring over her notes, just waiting for the defense case."

"You right. You ain't never lost to her though."

"No, not yet. But she knows what she's doing."

Lester leaned over and whispered in her ear. "Listen, from what I'm hearing, your man may be a bigger player than we thought."

"How so?"

"Word is, three dealers been shot dead in or near Barry Farms the last two months."

"Par for the course, these days."

"Yeah, but none of them's from Terrell's crew. He may be making moves. That or someone backing him is making moves."

"Glad things aren't getting complicated."

"I mean, we always wondered …"

"I know, but it's too late in the game for me to even think about that." She looked at the lockup list again, coughed, and cleared her throat. "Too many late-night Kools this week."

"Looks like you dressed for the closing."

"Way things are going, I should have worn black."

But he was right; she had dressed with the closing in mind. She'd chosen a simple but stylish dark red dress and gold bracelets that complemented her skin tone. She'd also had her hair done shortly before trial, keeping it natural and fairly short. As always, the goal was to look neat, professional, but not flashy.

"Listen, we're on a fifteen-minute recess, Judge Lake time, so I'd better go tell Terrell I'm not putting Dawan on the stand."

"Good luck with that, 'Net."

"Legal ethics 101. Thanks Lester, you done good."

*****

In the lockup, she stood beside the bars and stared down the marshal before turning to her client. The lawman moved five or six feet away from the cell, but even though she'd made him back off, it would be difficult to counsel Terrell without him hearing snatches of their conversation.

She braced herself as Terrell rose from his seat and approached her. *Black hands on silver bars again*; the phrase passed through her mind seconds before she noticed he'd rolled his shirtsleeves up, revealing the huge, melted-skin burn on his right forearm. A family history of sorts, etched on his arm. And another reason for the long-sleeved yellow shirt she'd dressed him in for the trial.

"Miss James," he began, "the robe say the case going to the jury, jus' like you said he would. Things don't seem to be looking too good. But it's our turn now, an we gonna need Dawan in there right away, turn things around for us."

"I'm afraid we have a problem."

"What you mean, a problem?"

"I'm not going to be able to call Dawan Turner as a witness."

"You got to be kiddin."

"Lester and I interviewed him, and we got the sense he, ah, wasn't there the night of the shooting."

"Oh no, he was there. I done *told* you he was there."

She moved closer to the bars.

"Thing is, we did a little digging and found out he was arrested the afternoon of the shooting for possession with intent to distribute. Over on Minnesota Avenue. Case was no-papered the following morning."

"No papered?"

"They dropped it."

Terrell flashed his boyish grin. "Hey, he's good to go then."

"No, he would have spent the night in the lockup. They release them in the morning. Which means he couldn't have seen the shooting."

"What the—goddamn! I'm sayin'—you got to call him, Dawan's our only witness to the crime. He saw it go down, he can say—"

She put her finger to her lips to signal him to speak quietly.

"Mr. Williams, I'm sorry but I can't do that. An attorney

is not allowed to call a witness she knows will testify falsely. There's nothing I can do about that."

He lowered his voice to a whisper. "Look, I need to tell you somethin' because— oh, man, I trusted you, and now …" He turned away from the bars, swore again and kicked the lockup's rusted bench with his foot.

She waited while he paced about the tiny space, hands pressed on his temples, as if the pressure would help him get a fix on the consequences of all she'd said. Then he took a breath, came back to the bars, and began again. "I'm telling you this because I know you worked hard on my case an I appreciate that. But you don't call Dawan, we done. Cause here's how it work. I get time for this, then I got to prove I'm still top dog even though I'm inside. You understand what I'm sayin'?"

"I think I follow you."

"I'm hoping you do. Cause I go down on this, on account of you don't call my man Dawan, that means someone got to be sent after you for that."

"You mean you would send someone, to … Oh. My God."

"I wouldn't if it was up to me, I swear, but the people I work with liable to tell me, 'Terrell: you show us you can do the payback thing on the lawyer, or someone else gonna step up an take your place.'" He shook his head and glanced at the marshal. "And then if I don't do nothing, who knows how it go for me in the house a correction."

She stood before him silently, trying to process all this before she took to words. He'd told her from the get-go he didn't shoot Kubic, but that he couldn't say who did or he'd be in trouble. That dilemma was starting to make more sense now.

"See if that's how it play out, an I get hard time, I'm jus' warning you, you liable to get somethin' hard too. Cause much as I like you, for what you done up to now, I got a business to run. An' like I said—you see what I'm sayin?"

"I'm afraid I do."

"So ... you best put my man on the stand, you know what's good for you, and everything be all right."

She shook her head, and he kicked the bars with his foot and swore. She flinched and moved back, and the marshal leapt to his feet.

"Sir," he said, "You sit down right now, or I'll have a word with the judge. And you'll be wearing chains the rest of your trial. Understood?"

Terrell gave the marshal a hard stare but took his seat. Then he focused on her again. "Miss James, you remember when I hired you I said I'd pay you up front, but if I went down you'd be the one to pay? You remember that?"

"You seemed to be joking, at the time."

"Yeah, cause I thought I'd walk, no problem. But now I'm thinking I might jus' have to fire you, and get me a new attorney, if I wanna beat this thing."

"Mr. Williams, you can tell the judge you'd like to fire me if you want to. Although we're pretty far into the trial so I don't know if—"

"Right, you don't know. But I do: if Dawan's not gonna testify, then I'll take the stand my own self and explain how I wasn't there that night."

"I'd suggest you not do that. You're not prepared for cross-examination, because we decided you weren't going to testify. Believe me, it'll be easy for the prosecutor to trip you up, make you angry, make you look bad. Plus, the jury will learn you have a conviction for possession of cocaine, because she'll be able to ask you all about it."

"I got a right to testify, don't I?"

"Yes, you do have that right. And it's your decision, not mine. But—"

"You jus' full a buts, ain't you."

Judge Lake's law clerk pushed the cellblock door open and stuck her head in the lockup. "Five minute warning," the young woman said, "then he's taking the bench again."

Annette waited until the clerk left and then tried again. "We stand a better chance if you don't testify. Kubic's ID is shaky, and his cross-examination went well—the jury already knows that in the grand jury, he described the shooter as wearing a red shirt. And we'll get that photo of you in your yellow shirt at Keisha's party—that same night—admitted during the defense case."

"But don't we need a witness who saw the shooter in the red shirt, for a really tight defense? Or are we jus' going with Keisha an' that reasonable doubt thing you keep talkin' about."

"Right. That's what we're shooting for, with Keisha and the shirt. If you take the stand or we call Dawan, things may come out that will hurt your case. Think it over, because we have to go back inside. Oh and please, make sure you roll your sleeves down before you go in the courtroom. The jury doesn't need to see that burn."

"You don't think if I testified I could—"

"No. But one thing you can do? Follow what's going on in the courtroom closely. Don't simply sit there. Watch like a hawk. If you're worried, look worried, so the jury knows you're worried."

"Ok, ok, I got it. But you don't use Dawan, and they come back 'guilty,' it's on you. Remember that."

"I hear you, Mr. Williams. See you inside."

"Got yourself a doozy," the marshal said as Annette opened the lockup door. She started to reply, then thought better of it. The one thing she seemed able to control today was her own mouth.

The first person she saw as she crossed the courtroom, heading for counsel table, was LaMont Jenkins, a/k/a "the Mont." Along the way, she'd heard he was Terrell's close friend and bodyguard. He was looking through the small window in the door to the courtroom, trying his best to gauge how things were playing out. Her stomach tightened a notch as she took her seat. Why had she decided to take this case in the first place? Months ago, it had made sense: the money was great, it was a triable high-stakes felony, and Terrell was entitled to a defense like everyone else. But as time went on and she'd learned more about her client, maybe she should have withdrawn.

"All rise," boomed the clerk, and Judge Lake strode into the room, took the bench, and looked at his watch. Then he reminded everyone court was back in session, the jury was waiting, and they were on the record.

"Let's get this show on the road, Miss James. How long do you think the defense case will take?"

"I'm not sure, at this point."

"Exactly what I thought you'd say."

"We're not required to reveal that information, Your Honor."

"I'll let that one pass. Let's get started."

She glanced at Terrell, who eyeballed her for a second, then turned away. "The defense is ready," she said, knowing that for the first time in the eight years she'd practiced criminal law, that wasn't the case.

*****

Annette began the defense case by introducing Terrell's party photo through Keisha, who swore he'd worn the yellow shirt he sported in the photo all that day. Then, after presenting records showing the shooting took place after sundown, on a corner without a working streetlight, Annette announced the defense had no further evidence—much to Judge Lake's surprise.

She hadn't called Dawan, despite what Terrell had said in the lockup, but so far so good. He wasn't making much eye contact, but he hadn't tried to fire her yet. And, he'd decided not to testify, having been told by the marshal that if he did and was convicted, Lake would assume he'd lied on the stand and jack up his sentence. Still, she couldn't shake the feeling the jury's verdict would impact her life as much as it would Terrell's.

By the time both sides rested, she felt the case was so close, the outcome would depend on whose closing argument was most convincing.

As always, the government went first. Annette fretted as Flynn delivered an even better closing than usual, managing to personify the community's outrage at the heinous crime that had been committed, thanking God Kubic hadn't died after taking four hits at close range, and pointing her finger at Terrell repeatedly as she argued he was guilty of attempted murder.

She took a moment, as Flynn covered some standard points prosecutors made in their closings, to fix the sequence of her own argument in her head. Hopefully, it would still be fixed there when it was her turn to face the jury.

After Flynn finished, Judge Lake said, "*Miss James*. Would you proceed, please."

Annette thought she detected a touch of annoyance in Lake's tone but decided not to raise the issue—the timing was bad. It was more important to respond to Flynn's argument immediately.

"Thank you, Your Honor," she said, and moved quickly to the heart of the arena—the ten-by-twelve-foot space before the jury box—hoping her demeanor communicated a sense of urgency and concern. Then she took a short, careful step closer to the box, looking to establish a degree of intimacy with its occupants without crowding their space. It was a practiced move.

She saw she had their full attention, and not just because she was about to deliver her closing. In the strange, unfathomable chemistry of the courtroom, her looks were an ingredient that aided her advocacy. It didn't hurt that she was slim, bronze-skinned, and thirty-three, or that—so friends told her—she sported a smile that made people want to know her better. All she knew was the combination of ingredients that made her who she was seemed to work, at least in this context, and she was grateful for that because she needed whatever help they might lend to her client's cause.

She let the silence linger a little longer so everyone in the box would feel the full significance of the moment. The importance this day played in the life of Mr. Williams. Next, she reminded herself her client had always maintained his innocence, and—threats or no threats—was entitled to her best effort. Then she inhaled and stood as tall and straight as she could and began.

"Now, we've all seen Mr. Kubic, and we know he has a terrible burden to bear for the rest of his life. And in asking you to find my client not guilty of firing the shots that injured him, the defense is not saying Earl Kubic is a bad person or minimizing the seriousness of his injuries. We are saying that while he's making a good-faith effort to identify the man who shot him—and honestly believes Terrell Williams was the gunman—he's mistaken: we have the wrong person on trial here.

"As Mr. Kubic told you, he was on the corner of Alabama and H that night in May, trying to pay the balance due on some cocaine he'd bought two weeks before. The money was overdue, and he was five hundred dollars short. But he knew if he did not pay back at least part of the money, the people he owed it to would come looking for him. So he was there trying to minimize the damage, and as the prosecutor said, it was courageous of him to do that."

Annette moved away from the jury box little by little, drifting toward counsel table as she spoke, so she stood behind Terrell and could place her hand on his shoulder as she continued. "But he identified Mr. Williams as the person who shot him. And that's why we're here today, isn't it?" A little contact, to send them a signal she wasn't afraid of him, so they shouldn't be either.

"Because what does the evidence show? It shows Earl Kubic got—at best—a split-second look at the man who shot him. Remember, the person who did the shooting was not the person who sold Kubic the drugs. The shooter was someone he didn't know. Hadn't seen before.

"Picture it: a crowded street corner on a hot spring night. Events are moving quickly. Mr. Kubic is talking with the dealer about the money he owes, that's his focus, and suddenly someone with a gun pushes through the crowd and shots ring out. Kubic falls to the ground, people are yelling and shouting, the shooter runs. The dealer runs. The question is, in the midst of that chaos, was he able to get a good enough look at the shooter to be able to identify him accurately? Or did he pick the wrong person?

"What was his initial description of the shooter? 'About twenty, heavy set, clean-shaven.' He did pretty good for a man in pain, a man who'd been shot several times, but you can't help but notice the lack of detail in that description, can you. What was the shooter wearing? How tall was he? How did he wear his hair?" She paused for a moment, as if waiting for the jurors to answer her questions, before making her point: "We don't know, because things happened too fast for Mr. Kubic to get a good look at the man who'd shot him."

She walked back to counsel table, picked up the handful of photos lying on it, and held them up to the jury. As she did so, she noticed the Mont and a white guy she didn't recognize, sitting in the back row of the spectator's section, and lost her train of thought for a few seconds.

"… But … you may be thinking, what about his photo identification, and then the lineup and his ID here in court? Doesn't that show Mr. Kubic was right?

"No. Because despite what Miss Flynn said, if Earl Kubic made a mistake two weeks after the shooting, when he picked my client's photo out of a group of pictures, he simply repeated that mistake at the lineup. And here again in court, before you."

Flynn yanked her head up and glared at Annette. She could feel the prosecutor's eyes on her but kept her focus on the jury. Nothing to be gained by glaring back. Instead, she left Terrell and moved from counsel table back to the well of the court, before the jury again.

"In fact, you've heard evidence that shows Mr. Kubic is making a mistake. Because when he testified under oath at the grand jury, he said he thought the person who shot him was wearing a red shirt. 'Things happened real fast, but I think the shooter was wearing a red shirt.' But as the evidence has shown, Terrell Williams was wearing a yellow shirt that night."

She stopped and gestured toward Terrell. Ideally, right now he would look scared. Like the stakes were high for him and he was frightened, not knowing what the jurors would do. Instead, he simply stared at the tabletop before him, as if his mind were on some other thing entirely. Some crucial business he needed to take care of when all this blew over. Inside, Annette sighed. Terrell was wearing a yellow shirt, but when it counted most he was not wearing the expression of an innocent man. There was nothing she could do about that, except move on to her next point—fast.

"So, members of the jury: doesn't the evidence show the real shooter wore red, while my client wore yellow? Red—yellow. That's a big difference. That's why I asked my client to wear a yellow shirt today. No one could mistake that shirt for a red shirt, am I right? And that means Mr. Kubic mistook Terrell Williams for the shooter.

"What difference does it make? It makes a reasonable doubt kind of difference. It's enough to give you a doubt—for which you can give a specific reason—about whether my client shot Mr. Kubic."

Annette was rolling now, almost in her groove, as she reminded the jurors of the government's heavy burden of proof, and that the defense had no obligation to present any evidence whatsoever—instead it could rest, and often did, when it was clear the government hadn't met its burden. Yet some primal part of her felt she wasn't convincing them, and she wasn't used to that. The red shirt was her trump card, all she had to work with really, and jurors one and seven didn't seem to think it was enough.

Nevertheless, it was time for the climax of the closing. She moved closer to the box, looked each juror briefly in the eye, and did her best to drive her argument home:

"So, ladies and gentlemen of the jury, the prosecution has not proved its case beyond a reasonable doubt. Instead, it relies totally on eyewitness testimony the evidence shows is unreliable, shows Mr. Kubic is mistaken, and is contradicted by Kubic's own description of the shooter. You're being asked to convict a man on the basis of a cross-racial identification, made long after dark, by a man under great stress."

She closed by stressing the government's heavy burden of proof and imploring the jurors to return a verdict of not guilty on all counts.

She walked back to her seat at counsel table slowly, head bowed to signal the solemnity of the moment, hoping her words would linger in the minds of the jurors while Flynn made her rebuttal. It wasn't her best closing. And she knew Flynn was fired up, hoping to nail the young man sitting twelve feet to her left. Hoping to remove him from the streets for a decade or more. "Kubic was lucky," she'd told Annette on the break, "Luckier than the others."

*****

Annette was used to hearing the words "not guilty" at the end of a trial. They washed over her like the warm waters of a relaxing spring, making the room glow, the jurors smile, and her client embrace her while the prosecutor slinked out of the courtroom. So she wasn't all that surprised to hear the jurors return a verdict of "not guilty" on the assault with intent to kill count. But when Lake asked for their verdict on the lesser included offense—assault with a dangerous weapon—the foreperson uttered the word "guilty," and its effect on her was seismic. The room seemed to spin for a moment; after that, everything seemed to proceed in slow motion.

She asked for a poll of the jurors, hoping one of them might have second thoughts, and tried her best to concentrate as each one of them repeated the word "guilty."

Judge Lake thanked them for their service, and they filed out of the room without looking at the defense table.

As Annette regained her focus, she reminded herself that nothing she experienced could match the impact of a guilty verdict on a defendant. The consequences were often measured in years, even decades, depending on the offense. And in Maximum John Lake's courtroom, the word "guilty" usually meant the statutory max. She reached out to Terrell to console him, but he pulled away from her, bowed his head and resumed staring at the oak table before him. A moment later, Judge Lake told him to "please step back with the marshal, sir," and the marshals escorted him back to the lockup, where he'd trade his shirt and slacks in for a jumpsuit.

After the Mont and the other spectators left the courtroom, she packed her briefcase and waited a few minutes to allow Terrell time to change and compose himself. Then she went back to his cell to try and explain the consequences to him.

"What's done is done," he said, waving her away, "so don't bother, jus'—shut it."

"Hear me out a minute," she said, doing her best to keep any trace of emotion out of her voice. "I'm sorry things didn't work out—it was a tough case. At least we beat the lead count in the indictment. The fifteen-year count."

"Yeah, so now I'm jus' facing ten years on the back side of the bars for the dangerous weapon. Ain't that a bitch. 'Specially when everyone promised me I would walk."

"I never said that. I never said—"

"I hired you cause people said you was so good you'd keep me on the street 'til trial and then beat the charges—and I expected you to do jus' that. Matter a fact, if you'd a put Dawan on the stand like I told you to, I'd be a free man now. But you didn't and now look."

"I think—"

"You don't call a witness says I didn't do it, that's ineffective resistance of counsel. So I'm thinking you need to be fired, and I need to hire myself a new lawyer for the sentencing. You best leave outa here right now, cause you—you in big trouble."

Annette had expected him to be upset, but despite his earlier threat had hoped not to be fired, given his acquittal on the attempt murder count and the amount of lawyer magic she'd done for him pretrial.

She had to ask: "Mr. Williams, are you really planning to send someone after me?"

She waited as he took a deep breath.

"... I don't know. I should, I really should, cause ... look I can't talk about that now."

He turned away from her.

"All right. Again, I'm sorry about the verdict. We'll talk soon."

"Yeah, *talk*. ... Right."

She knew not to prolong their conversation at this point, so said she'd be in touch and left him alone to work through his rage.

The level of anger he'd displayed upset her, but as she

made her way through the silent courtroom, she tried to discount his threats, telling herself they had come at an emotional time and that no client is more ungrateful for a defense attorney's work than one headed for the pale blue prison bus after the verdict.

At first, she decided she'd wait a day or two, then try to visit him at the jail and work things out. Usually, convicted clients calmed down after a few days in the slammer, and turned to talking about their appeal. But the knot in her stomach signaled this time might be different.

It suddenly seemed like a good idea to spend the weekend visiting her sister in New York. Hang out a few days, until she found out if he'd fired her and retained another lawyer. If he hadn't, then she'd return and try to visit him at the jail—but if he didn't show for the visit, it would mean he'd followed through on his threat, and her life was in danger. In which case, then what? Go to the police? This was new territory, and she wasn't sure what to do.

Right now she was too tired to sort it all out. It had been a long day, and it was time to decompress—maybe take Lester out for a drink. No, what was she thinking, what a brain-fried idea! Heading home and locking the doors would be a far better choice. Then she'd pack, call a cab, and head for the airport: there was nothing else to do at this point but run.

Acknowledgments

The author would like to thank Sarah, Kelly, Joshua, and the rest of the fine staff at Gatekeeper Press for their assistance, creativity, and attention to detail. Heartfelt thanks also to Mary Beth Lerner, Kevin Clarke, A.X. Ahmad, Terri Shuck, Howard O'Leary, and Michael Carey for their support, and for the valuable input they shared with me along the way.

www.ingramcontent.com/pod-product-compliance
Lightning Source LLC
LaVergne TN
LVHW041634060526
838200LV00040B/1561